PLAYER ON ICE

PLAYER ON ICE

BOYS OF WINTER #5

S.R. GREY

Player on Ice (Boys of Winter #5)
Copyright © 2018 by S.R. Grey

ISBN-10: 0-9979749-8-2 (e-book version)
ISBN-13: 978-0-9979749-8-0 (e-book version)

ISBN-10: 0-9979749-9-0 (print version)
ISBN-13: 978-0-9979749-9-7 (print version)

Editing: Hot Tree Editing
Proofreading: Deaton Author Services
Cover Photographer: CJC Photography
Model: Matt Ricker
Cover Design: Najla Qamber
Interior Design and Formatting: by:
www.emtippettsbookdesigns.com

OTHER BOOKS BY
S.R. GREY

Boys of Winter series
Destiny on Ice
Resistance on Ice
Complications on Ice
Caution on Ice
Player on Ice

Judge Me Not series
I Stand Before You
Never Doubt Me
Just Let Me Love You
The After of Us

Inevitability duology
Inevitable Detour
Inevitable Circumstances

Promises series
Tomorrow's Lies
Today's Promises

A Harbour Falls Mystery trilogy
Harbour Falls
Willow Point
Wickingham Way

Laid Bare novella series
Exposed: Laid Bare 1
Unveiled: Laid Bare 2
Spellbound: Laid Bare 3
Sacrifice: Laid Bare 4

I FUCK UP ROYALLY

JAXON

With three minutes left in the final period of an elimination game, our hockey team—the Las Vegas Wolves—is down 2-1.

"Don't worry, boys!" I yell to my left and right wingers as we hop over the boards and onto the ice for our shift. "We got this."

I'm excited that my line could save the day. With me centering, where I can make key passes to my linemates, we have an excellent chance of scoring and sending this game into overtime. Hell, we'd better score, and soon, or our second run in two years for the holy grail of hockey, the motherfucking Stanley Cup, is over.

Done, *finito*—as in this is it.

That's right, this is game number seven, the second round of the playoffs, and we *must* win in order to stay alive. Otherwise, we Wolves are looking at a summer spent on the links.

No way. I don't even fucking like golf!

"Heads up," Noel Sandlund, a defenseman and good friend of mine, calls out. "Quit fucking daydreaming, Jaxon."

Shit, he's right. I'm not focused.

What's wrong with me?

And just like that, it goes from bad to worse. Everything feels like it's happening in slow motion, though not in any kind of good way. No, this is more like those nightmares where things move all sludgy-like and you can't react in time to anything.

Like now—the puck's heading my way, and my stick's on the ice, but I'm at a weird angle and can't correct in time.

Of course, the puck zooms right past me.

Fuck, this is worse than a nightmare.

Capitalizing on my screw-up, a forward from the Edmonton Oilers—that's the team we're playing against—skates off with the puck meant for me.

And with that, I just fucked up royally.

But wait, I can still fix this.

Spinning around, I skate off as quickly as I can to catch up with Puck Stealer.

Shit, the bastard's heading straight for our unprotected net.

We pulled the goaltender seconds ago and this prick somehow just evaded a winger *and* Dylan Culderway, a really good defenseman who's now on the ice.

No worries, I'll save the day.

I'll back-check this prick and regain control. The puck needs to be back in *their* zone, not ours, since time is ticking away like sand through an hourglass.

Speaking of which, how much time *is* left?

I glance up at the Jumbotron and find there's 1:47 left in the game. *Better move quickly.*

But wait, I lost seconds peering up at the board and now my guy's getting away.

That can't happen!

I skate fast, reaching for Puck Stealer with my stick and praying I don't get called for hooking this late in the game.

But when my blade gets hung up in the opponent's jersey the whistle blows.

Great, I'm getting called for a penalty.

I, Jaxon Holland, have singlehandedly just fucked up any chance of the Wolves tying the game.

Angry at my own stupidity, I skate over to the penalty box, unable to meet any of my teammates' accusing eyes.

Slamming my stick down once I'm in the box, I grind out a disgruntled, "Shit, fuck, damn."

Like that's going to help.

It won't, and now that I'm here in the sin bin, I'm pretty much helpless for the rest of the game. Cringing, I have to watch as the Oilers go on a power play, thanks to me.

Of course, they score a fucking goal.

My penalty is over, but it's too late.

I skate dejectedly over to the bench, feeling so guilty, so horrible. Everyone is quiet, even Coach Townsend, who usually has plenty to say.

Watching the remaining time tick away is pure torture.

Our top line of Brent Oliver, Nolan Solvenson, and Benny Perry are out on the ice. But it's a lost cause. There just isn't enough time to make something happen, especially because the Oilers have gone into full lockdown defensive mode.

When they win the game, they celebrate like crazy on the ice.

Shit, that should be us, I think to myself.

I hate that we have to wait around to shake hands. It's worse because we're in Edmonton and their fans are going nuts.

Me, I just want to disappear to the locker room. But since I can't, I peer up into the stands to pass the time.

Bad move.

First thing I see is a sign someone has already made that reads **The Fans Thank Jaxon Holland for Zoning Out. Not Once but Twice!**

No!

There's even a little stick drawing of me, hooking the Oiler.

Then I catch sight of another sign. This one has a stick-figure of me staring up at the Jumbotron, looking lost in thought.

Ugh!

There's no doubt that these signs are of me, seeing as both little cartoon guys are wearing number 23.

And to think I've really loved this season that that number was mine, only because I'm 23 years-old.

Get it, 23 on 23?

Oh, never mind.

Just then I spot yet *another* sign mocking my screw-up, this one depicting me bungling the puck.

What the hell?

Do these fans carry markers and poster board around with them? I always thought the signs were made at home and then brought to the arena. I guess not all fans do it that way.

In any case, fuck my life.

And fuck it even more since I'm now noticing teammates of mine looking up, reading those very same signs.

Great.

Like they need another reminder of who flaked out and failed the team.

When we finally make it back to the locker room, after a handshake session that seems to last forever, things go from bad to worse. Strangers hating on me is one thing, but my own teammates ignoring me like I'm a pariah hurts like hell.

I want so badly to tell them I'm sorry. But why bother? Words mean nothing and they know it. My time to shine was when I was on the ice. Too bad I flaked and blew the game.

I deserve this silent treatment.

So I take it like a man.

Finally, though, someone does talk to me—Noel Sandlund. He's Dylan's defensive partner, my friend, and a pretty cool guy overall.

He's taking his gear off in the stall next to me when he quietly states, "Hey, buck up, Holland. The guys will get over this."

I snort out a *yeah-right* guffaw. "Sure they will. Hell, I won't be surprised if they petition over the summer to have me traded."

Snorting, Noel counters, "No way, man. You're the best second-line center around. And we all know it."

"Thanks," I sigh. "That means a lot. Too bad I wasn't at my best tonight, though, not when it mattered."

"Hey, shit happens."

"It sure does. But it's always at the worst times, eh?"

"That's just the way it goes, Holland."

"You're not kidding."

Some other guys take notice of us talking and, to my relief, the ice begins to thaw. Pun totally intended.

By the time we're boarding the team jet, things are almost back to normal.

During the flight back to Las Vegas, a few guys ask me if I'd like to play cards with them.

I say yes, and though it's a little tense at first, soon we're all laughing and joking like old times.

Phew!

I breathe a sigh of relief.

Everything is going to be okay.

But then we touch down, and all hell breaks loose.

2

MR. HOCKEYPANTS

CARA

"**N**oooo, how can you be so stupid, Jaxon Holland?"

That's me, screaming at the TV. Why? Because the Las Vegas Wolves' usually hockey-smart center just did the dumbest thing—he hooked a player and got called for a penalty...with less than two minutes left in this playoff elimination game!

"What in the world was he thinking?" I smack my head, like maybe this might telepathically knock some sense into Jaxon. "This is a do-or-die game, dude," I ramble on. "Are you high? Taking a dumb penalty like that?"

I know Holland's not impaired in any way, but zoning out at the most critical point in the game does make him look like he might be trying out to be an extra in a new *Cheech & Chong* remake.

Plus, this is not his first airhead mistake.

He missed a perfectly passed puck from Brent Oliver seconds ago, and then lost track of the guy who capitalized on it. And why would Jaxon do that? Because Stoner Boy was too busy peering up at the Jumbotron.

But this—a hooking penalty, with hardly any time left in regulation? If that's not the act of someone who's high, I don't know what is.

"Seriously, dude, put down the bong," I mutter.

Hey, wait!

I think I just came up with the perfect angle for my next blog post, something that'll grab the attention of my followers. You have to keep things interesting, you know, and a hook like that is sure to please.

That's why my blog is a success.

That's right. I'm not just a rabid Wolves fan; I'm also the secret mastermind behind a super-successful hockey blog known as *Mr. Hockeypants.*

And it's time to write tonight's post, while it's still fresh in my mind.

Hurrying off to the only bedroom in my small but cozy apartment, I retrieve my tablet.

By the time I return to the living room, the opposing team has scored.

"Noooo..." I slump down on the sofa.

Just like that, the Wolves' season is over.

"That's just great," I grumble. "Game over. Stoner-wannabe Jaxon Holland has officially lost it for us."

Okay, maybe it wasn't his fault entirely. The whole team was flat tonight. But those critical errors he made in the final minutes are all I can think about. Every fan out there will be looking for a scapegoat, so it may as well be Holland.

Anger and irritation fuel my every move, as evidenced with the way I roughly pin up my long auburn hair and bang on the screen to log in.

This post is going to be a doozy, as I plan to skewer the hell out of Holland.

I do feel a little bad. I like Jaxon. I don't know him personally or anything, but he seems nice enough in interviews. Plus, and this may be the most important reason of all, he's über cute. If I had to vote for the hottest player on the Wolves, I'd definitely cast my ballot for Jaxon.

I like his sandy brown hair and how it always appears mussed up, like he just rolled out of bed. And his striking emerald green eyes are stunning. Everyone talks about how pretty they are. Add in his firm, muscular body and Jaxon is the perfect fantasy man.

Well, he's *my* perfect fantasy man.

Too bad for him *I'm* not writing the blog post. Mr. Hockeypants, my secret alter ego, is. And he lusts for no one.

He also doesn't pull any punches. He tells it like it is. He posts about all the teams, but mostly he writes about the Wolves since they're based in Las Vegas, where I live.

Mr. Hockeypants is hard on the players, no doubt about that. And as a result, many of the Wolves' players don't like him or the blog.

Oh, well, too bad. The things they hate are what people love.

Before I get started on composing tonight's sure-to-be-scathing post, I check out a few hockey-centric message boards to get a feel for the prevailing sentiment on the game.

Not surprisingly, the fans are as angry as I am at Jaxon.

That's fine. It's my duty to vent for them. If I rile them up in the process, so be it.

I'm not this harsh in real life. I'm actually pretty nice. This is just my shtick for the blog. That's why nobody would ever suspect that *I'm* Mr. Hockeypants. When people think of me, they think *oh, that sweet, friendly Cara Milne.*

Ha, if they only knew the truth.

And just what does Mr. Hockeypants have to say about tonight's debacle of a game?

Oh, a lot.

And it starts like this…

Hey, how about putting down the bong, #23. Not to accuse you of toking up or anything, before or during the game, but hell, it's the only reason Mr. Hockeypants can think of for why you screwed up all over the ice tonight.

Zoning out on a critical pass and being so enamored of the big bright Jumbotron above you, so much so that you let the guy you were responsible for get away with the puck, is just unacceptable.

And don't even get me started on that stupid penalty you brought onto yourself!

What's a fan supposed to think?

I'll tell you, bud. <-- "bud," hee-hee.

This fan suspects you took one hit too many, and I don't mean out on the ice. Now sure, we can all agree the illuminated big screen can look really pretty, and be distracting, but you'd think with you living in Las Vegas, you'd be immune to bright lights.

Guess not, seeing as I hear you don't spend much time outdoors. Word on the street is you much prefer the darkened strip clubs around town to the neon jungle.

Is that true, Jaxon?

Are you really that much of a dog?

Let's put it to the test, shall we?

Squirrel!

Giggling, I go on to recap the game, but with far less vitriol for the other players. I feel crappy placing so much responsibility for the loss on Jaxon, as I'm sure he'll receive even more negative attention from the fans after this post goes live, but you know what?

Jaxon Holland is a hockey player.

He's tough and can take it.

As I'm putting the finishing touches on my post—or should I say Mr. Hockeypants's post—my phone dings, indicating that I have a text.

It's my best friend, Noelle Sandlund, demanding that I call her ASAP.

Guess I better see what she wants. After all, it could be secret info on the game.

Noelle doesn't know it, but she's my covert inside contact for all things Wolves-related. That's how I knew about Jaxon and the strip clubs. Noelle doesn't work directly for the organization, but she's related to someone who does—her twin brother, defenseman Noel Sandlund.

Blowing out a breath, I hit Call.

Noelle answers right away with a sad-sounding, "Cara?"

"Hey, what's up? Is everything all right?"

"No it's not," she groans. "Didn't you watch that sorry excuse for a game? It was God awful, I swear. I still feel sick even now."

"I saw it, yes," I say, sighing in commiseration. "And I feel pretty gross about it myself."

Is that really why you feel sick? a little internal voice taunts.

"Oh, hush," I whisper.

I type with more vigor, covering up my words and finishing up my blog post.

Noelle, of course, notices. "Hey, what's going on over there? It sounds like you're doing…something."

"Oh, um, I-I...," I stammer. *Get it together, get it together.* "I was just thinking about the game, that's all. It really was a heartbreaker."

There, that sounds believable.

"It really was," Noelle agrees. "And I just don't know who to blame the most."

Er, I have an idea.

I, of course, don't say *that* out loud. What I do instead is toss the tablet onto the coffee table so I can pay full attention to Noelle. I just can't take a chance on slipping up again since she doesn't know I'm Mr. Hockeypants.

And she must never find out.

Even if I swore her to secrecy, she could inadvertently divulge to her brother that I'm the person behind the blog the Wolves love to loathe.

And we can't have that, right?

No.

So I need to tread carefully and not blame Jaxon Holland for this huge loss. Once I publish tonight's post, Noelle could see it and put two and two together. After all, *everyone* reads Mr. Hockeypants.

Trying to sound pensive, I state, "Just don't blame anyone then, Noelle. Or better yet, blame them all."

"Yeah, I guess," she says, sighing. "Though you have to admit, Jaxon Holland looked like total crap tonight."

Here we go...

Play it cool, play it cool.

"Hmm..." I pause as if I'm still lost in thought. "Yes, he made some mistakes, but it wasn't just him out there on the ice. The whole team played like shit."

Noelle is quiet for a beat, then softly says, "I didn't realize you were such a Jaxon Holland fan, Cara."

"Um, I'm not. I mean, I am, but that's not why I'm defending him. I just think everyone on the team bears responsibility when you have a loss like that."

"Yeah, maybe," she muses. "Mistakes were made by everyone, that's true."

Now that I have her back on-track, I say, "Yeah, the Wolves didn't generate nearly enough offense early on. You can't get behind, not even by one goal, in a game like that."

"Still, Cara, Holland had a chance to tie things up and blew it. What a time to fuckup, right?"

I'm quick to maintain, "Sure, but in the end it's the whole team's fault for the loss."

Noelle laughs. "Wow, I think you might be the only person in this whole town giving Jaxon a pass right now."

If only she knew.

"Wait, Cara, you don't have a crush on him, do you?"

Okay, now she's talking crazy.

"Please," I scoff.

"You have to admit, he is pretty hot."

"Irrelevant," I scoff.

She ignores me and says, "I could ask Noel to introduce you sometime."

This girl is relentless!

I sputter and cough at the absurdity of such a thing. Can you imagine? Jaxon Holland set up on a date with Mr. Hockeypants?

What if we really liked each other?

Pfft, that'd be crazy.

Not to mention, I'd feel like the biggest jerk on the planet if he ever really liked me.

So, yeah, no.

Emphatically, I state, "No way would I ever go out with that guy. It would never work, Noelle."

"Why not?" she asks. "I actually think you two would make a cute couple."

Sweet baby Jesus, make her stop.

"Can we please just talk about something else?" I beg.

Relenting, she says, "Sure, like what?"

I scramble to come up with something other than Jaxon, but since hockey is still on my mind, I end up asking, "Is there anything new with Noel?"

"I haven't talked to him today at all," Noelle replies. "But he said yesterday that if the Wolves lost this game, he's going to be heading over to Sweden to play for Team USA in the hockey world championships."

I welcome the subject change, and say, "Oh, wow, that's cool. Didn't your great-grandparents come from Sweden? Maybe Noel can look up history on your family tree while he's over there."

"Yeah, they did," Noelle confirms. "And I hope he does just that. I only wish I could go with him. Not to go all Ancestry.com or anything, but I could use some time away. Knowing I was passed over for that summer internship I really wanted freaking blows."

Noelle is working on her MBA and was in the running for a fantastic internship with a huge tech company.

Sadly, though, she didn't get it.

"I still call bullshit on that one," I say, rallying for my friend. "You were definitely the better candidate."

It was down to two women, and Noelle was certain she had it in the bag. But at the last minute, the company went with the other candidate.

"Whatever," she sighs. "Maybe you and I should just say 'fuck it' and go somewhere."

"What do you mean?" I query. "Like go on a vacation?"

"Yeah, Cara. Why not?"

"It's not a bad thought," I muse. "And Lord knows I'm always up for traveling. Hmm, maybe we should."

I think about how hard I worked this hockey season to make the Mr. Hockeypants blog a success. And I did just that. Quite an accomplishment considering it was my first stab ever at blogging.

But with the Wolves out of the playoff picture, I can now relax a little. Since they're my primary focus, I won't have nearly as much to chat about.

"You know what?" I say at last. "No maybes about it. A vacation is a great idea. You want to get away, and I could use a little time off myself."

Since Noelle doesn't know about the blog, I'm not surprised when she says, "Uh, no offense, but you could use a little time off from what exactly?"

Eek, think fast.

"Oh, just work," I say.

Crap, that's not a good response. She's going to be really confused now.

Sure enough, she says, "Work, Cara? But you don't even have a job."

Noelle's not being rude. It's true. I don't work outside of the blog. And all she's aware of is that I inherited a tidy sum of money, in the form of a trust fund, from my grandfather when he passed away a couple of years ago. That's how I originally paid for my apartment, car, etc. But now Mr. Hockeypants takes care of those things.

If only Noelle knew hockey pays for my bills, just like it does for her brother.

Too bad I can't tell her.

So, instead, casually I say, "Hmm, good point on the no job. Still, it'd be nice to get away."

"It would," she agrees.

"So where should we go?"

"Oh, I know the perfect place, Cara. And the best part is it won't cost us a penny besides airfare."

I laugh. "Wait, that sounds too good to be true."

"It's not," she assures me. "Guess you forgot all about Noel's beach house. It's available for the whole summer now that he's going to Sweden."

"Holy crap," I exclaim. "I did forget all about that place."

Noelle's brother owns the sweetest beach house known to man. It's on a freaking private island off the coast of Florida and it is *spectacular.*

"So what do you think?" she asks. "We could fly down in a day or two and stay as long as we like."

"Um," I say, hesitating. "I don't want to be a downer, but shouldn't you ask Noel first?"

"Nah, he'll be too busy over the next couple of days. I'll just tell him once we're down there. Trust me, he's not going to mind."

From all I've heard, Noel is a pretty laid-back guy, so I go with Noelle's instinct on this one.

"Well," I state, "guess I better start packing."

"Definitely, and I'll get things set up. I just need to call down there ahead of time and make sure Noel's staff knows to stock food and essentials for us."

Impressed and a little awed, I remark, "Wow, your brother has a staff?"

"He does indeed. But don't be too impressed. It's just a groundskeeper and a housekeeper who check in every couple of weeks. You know, like for basic upkeep since Noel's not there much."

"Hmm, I see."

"Oh wait, I just thought of something else. I'll have them stock liquor too. We can't lie out on the beach without little umbrella drinks, right?"

"Definitely not," I agree. "Perish the thought."

She laughs. "So, do you have any special requests?"

I think it over and come up with only one— "Could you ask someone to stock a couple fifths of vodka?"

"Ooh, that's right. I forgot your favorite drink in the world is Sex on the Beach. So yeah, sure"—I hear pen-to-paper and conclude that Noelle is taking down notes—"we're going to need vodka."

Damn. I sigh. It's been so long for me that I kind of wish another kind of Sex on the Beach was in the cards, like *actual* sex on the beach. That'd never happen on this trip, though. The island is too secluded and far too private. It'll just be me and Noelle down there, with an occasional appearance from the staff. Anyone else on the island will most likely be a worker, as well.

I realize then that Noelle is in the middle of asking me something.

"Wait, what?" I say. "I'm sorry. I didn't catch that."

"I was just asking you what you were thinking about," she says. "It sounded like I'd lost you there for a minute."

"Oh, you did," I confess. "I was dreaming of turquoise waters and island breezes."

And sex, I don't add.

"It'll be more than that," she replies. "We're going to have lots of fun, Cara. You'll see. This is going to be a trip to remember."

Somewhere deep inside, I get this all-consuming feeling that it *will* be a trip to remember, maybe even the kind that changes an entire life.

3

WANNA GET AWAY?

JAXON

I feel like I'm living in one of those Southwest Airlines commercials. You know the ones, where they ask if you... "Wanna get away?"

Yes, yes I do!

I want to get as far away from Las Vegas as I can. I've got reporters calling me like crazy, and irate fans mailing me stuffed squirrels and fake fucking bongs.

Too bad those aren't real. I'm ready to light up anything mind-numbing at this point.

And it's all fucking Mr. Hockeypants's fault!

I'd like to kick that dude's ass. He made a bad situation a hundred times worse with his dumbass blog post. I swear if I ever get my hands on that guy, whoever he is, it's not going to be pretty.

Too bad his damn identity is a total mystery.

Trust me, though. I'm going to eventually uncover the man behind that keyboard.

And when I do…

But for now, I simply need to get away. That's why I plan on taking a nice, long vacation.

I just don't know where to go.

"I'm open to suggestions *and* traveling companions," I told my teammates the other day when we were all cleaning out our lockers for the summer.

So far, there've been no takers in the traveling companion department. No one is mad at me anymore, but everyone's too busy with their own lives. Brent has his wedding with Aubrey coming up in Minnesota this summer, and he and Nolan have plans to fly up early to get in some fishing and quality bro time.

Benny is busy with Eliza and her daughter. And Dylan and his new wife, Chloe, have a baby on the way. A lot of the other guys are playing in the world championships over in Sweden, including my good friend Noel.

So I'm on my own.

I look up dozens of potential vacation destinations on my phone, but nothing calls to me. Maybe I need to be like my parents and find myself a good old-fashioned travel agency. I remember when I was a kid how they used to return with big, glossy brochures depicting cool, exotic locales. Maybe browsing through the pages of one of those, as opposed to scanning around on the internet, will yield better results.

So I search for a local travel agency, one with a real office and everything. It's not easy, though, as the internet has made most obsolete.

At last, though, I come upon an address for one in a nearby mall.

Perfect.

I make the short drive over.

Unfortunately it's a Saturday afternoon and the mall is a madhouse. I'm bound to get recognized if I don't take precautions.

Feeling like an undercover agent, which is kind of cool, I slip on a ball cap and pull it low over my eyes. Then I slide on a pair of sunglasses.

All set…or maybe not.

Seems my undercover attempt is all for naught since, as I'm stepping out of my flashy sports car, someone yells over, "Hey, it's him. Jaxon Holland. You fucker, you really blew it for us."

Another heckler chimes in, "You suck, Holland. I hope the Wolves trade you during the off-season. What are you doing at the mall, anyway? Isn't there a strip club somewhere that you'd rather go to?"

Damn it. That fucking Mr. Hockeypants! I haven't even been to a strip club in over a month.

I really want to scream something back to my hecklers, but I know the rules—never engage. You'll always lose in the end.

The fans are still so angry. I should probably scrap the travel agency idea, as I'm sure it'll be worse inside the mall.

So I hop back in my car, grateful that I have tinted windows.

I'm about to speed away, but then Noel calls.

Hitting the Bluetooth button on the steering wheel, I grind out a strained, "Yeah?"

"Whoa, dude, what's wrong?" he asks. "You sound kind of stressed."

"Fuck, man, I am. I'm in the mall parking lot being heckled by irate fans."

"Wow. That sucks."

"You're not kidding. I need to get the fuck out of this city for a while, give these nutty people a chance to cool off."

Noel replies, "Say no more. It's your lucky day, Holland."

Just then someone tosses a stuffed squirrel onto my windshield, and I mutter back a dejected, "Hmm, I don't know about that."

"No, listen," he goes on, "that's why I'm calling. I just remembered when we were cleaning out our lockers that you said you wanted to get away. I don't know why I didn't think of it sooner, but I have the perfect place where you can go to and be totally left alone."

"Ah, that sounds like heaven, my friend."

Someone walks by my car just then, laughing and pretending to toke up.

"Dude," I sigh. "Anywhere is better than here, so long as there are no Wolves fans."

Noel chuckles and assures me, "Not a one will be where I'm thinking, I promise. This place is a tropical island, and the house on it is privately owned."

"Wait, are you talking about your beach house?"

"I sure am," Noel confirms.

Noel's beach house is on a tiny island off the coast of Florida. Some other rich people have houses there too, but they're never really around. That means not only would there be no Wolves fans like he said, but there'd be pretty much no one around at all.

"Dude, you just totally made my day. No, wait, I think you made my whole week. Hell, you made my fucking month!"

Noel laughs. "Cool, because you can stay there that long and more. The house is yours for the whole summer, if you want."

"Are you fucking kidding me?"

Just then there's a knock on my window. It's a teenybopper girl, holding up a piece of paper.

"Hold on a sec," I say to Noel. "I think someone wants an autograph."

Finally, a nice fan!

"No problem," Noel says.

I power down the window and the girl smiles sweetly at me.

See, she really is nice.

"Sorry to bug you, sir," she says. "But you're Jaxon Holland, right?"

She doesn't strike me as the harassing type, so I let down my guard.

"Yes, yes, I am, miss."

"Oh, perfect." Shoving the piece of paper at me, which I take, she says, "Can you autograph this?"

"Yeah, sure... Hey, wait a second." I peer down at the paper in disbelief. "Is this a printout of Mr. Hockeypants's blog post? Who would want this crap signed?"

Giggling, she replies, "I do. Is that okay? You gotta love Mr. Hockeypants, right? He just tells it like it is."

"Sure he does," I mutter as I sign my name across words I'm convinced were written purely to fuck with my life.

I hand the paper back to the girl, and she runs off.

"Wow, that was weird," I remark.

Noel is still on the line and says, "I heard all of that. Sorry, man."

I shake my head. "Can you believe my life these days?"

Before Noel can respond, I notice where the girl has run off to. And it's not to the mall, or to her car. She's stopped at a news van, where she's handing over the paper I just autographed.

"Oh, fuck!"

"What now?" Noel asks.

"That autograph I just signed is for a fucking news story. This is horrible, man. It's going to be plastered all over the media that I just autographed a hit piece on me. That's like me agreeing to everything that dickwad Hockeypants dude wrote. What the hell was I thinking?"

Noel, in a low voice, says, "Uh, about that beach house—"

"Fuck, man, say no more. Drop off the keys as soon as you can. I am outta here."

ISLAND SURPRISE

CARA

Noel Sandlund's beach house exceeds all expectations. It's a funky white contemporary with lots of floor-to-ceiling windows that showcase stunning views of the ocean. They also give the home a real open-air feel.

As I walk from room to beautiful room, I can't believe this gorgeous abode is all mine and Noelle's for the next few weeks. That's how long she and I have decided to stay. Although we may extend our vacation longer if we really like it here. It's not like I have anything I need to be back for, and since Noelle didn't get that internship she's free the whole summer too.

Speaking of Noelle...

"I can't wait for her to get here," I murmur as I plop down on a creamy white sectional sofa.

Beautiful as this place is, it's kind of boring hanging here all alone. I made a light dinner a while ago and checked out the outdoor patio off the living room. I even unpacked and chose a bedroom from the many available upstairs. But the truth is that I'm running out of things to do. I just want Noelle here so we can laugh and talk and get started on our island fun.

Ugh, where is she?

We were supposed to fly down together, but some last-minute grad school business held her up. The dean wanted to meet with her. It was something supposedly urgent, so it's not like she could blow it off.

While Noelle stayed behind, I hopped on our originally planned early morning flight. She rescheduled for the afternoon, but it's nine in the evening now and still no Noelle.

She should definitely be here by now. Come to think of it, it's kind of weird I've received no texts or calls from her all day.

Suddenly apprehensive that something's gone wrong, I grab my phone and call her. To my relief, she answers right away.

"Oh, thank God," I breathe out. "I was starting to think the dean may have kidnapped you."

She snorts, "If you saw how tiny the dean is, you'd never think that. I could probably take him down in under a minute."

Noelle is really tall and doesn't put up with any bullshit, so I reply, "I have no doubt." Then I get down to business. "Where in the hell are you, anyway? You don't sound like you're in transit."

"That's because I'm not," she says.

"What do you mean you're not? Was your flight delayed or something?"

"Oh, jeez, I don't even know."

Alarmed, I tell her, "Hey, you're scaring me here."

Laughing, she assures me, "It's nothing to be scared about, Cara. And I am sorry. I should've called or texted an update, but I've been running around like crazy since this morning. I literally just walked out of an interview two minutes ago."

Totally confused now, I murmur, "An interview? But it's like six o'clock back there. What are you talking about? Wasn't your meeting with the dean really early?"

"It was. But what he wanted to talk about was this interview I just came out of. He set it up for me."

"I am so lost right now," I say, feeling, well…lost.

With a note of apology in her tone, Noelle says, "I know and again, I'm sorry. If it's any consolation, my head's spinning too. But really, this is a good development."

Noelle then fills me in on how the meeting with the dean was in regard to that sweet internship she was vying for. Apparently, the candidate who was chosen backed out at the last minute.

"And since I was second in line," she continues, "they requested to speak with me as soon as possible."

Even though I'm disappointed she's clearly not en route, I'm amped for her.

"Well, don't leave me in suspense," I say excitedly. "What happened?"

"I got the internship!" she squeals.

"That is so awesome, Noelle. I'm truly happy for you."

"Um, you may not be, though, when you hear the bad part."

"Uh-oh, I think I know where this is going."

And I do. If she got the internship, she obviously can't be a beach bum for the next few weeks.

Sure enough, she informs me, "I won't be able to come down to the island. They want me to start right away."

Sure, I'm disappointed, but I'm thrilled for my best friend. Her dream internship has come through after all. How cool is that?

"Aw, that's okay," I say. "I can just go re-pack my things and book a flight back for tomorrow."

"Oh, no," she replies, "don't do that. Just stay down there as long as you like. Enjoy the beach and the sun, and hey, have a few cocktails for me. While you're out catching rays, you can think of how I'm back here in my sunless cubicle slaving away."

I'm tempted by her offer to stay, but hesitant.

"I don't know, Noelle. What would I do here on the island all by myself? I was already bored before I called you, and that was after only a few hours."

"Yeah, but this was just your first day, Cara. And you know how it is when you arrive at a new place. You have to acclimate, get used to your new surroundings."

"True," I agree.

And then I glance around and murmur, "Your brother's place *is* really nice."

"So stay. Better to be bored at a nice beach house than be bored sitting around your little apartment, right?"

"You do have a point," I concede. "But do you think Noel will be cool with me staying here without you?"

She scoffs, "Pfft, of course. He texted me earlier that he made it to Sweden, but I haven't had a chance to talk with him and update him on what's been going on. He doesn't know about the internship, or that anyone's at the beach house. But don't worry. I'll let him know that you're there and will be staying for a while."

"You sure it's okay?" I double-check.

"Yes, definitely. Now stop. Noel will be thrilled someone is enjoying his place and it's not just sitting there empty like always."

I think it over. Some time alone might be good for me. I can relax and be a beach bum on my own. Plus, hello, we're talking island paradise here. I'd be crazy to fly back.

I'm leaning toward staying, but to confirm my decision I slide open the glass doors to the patio and lean against the frame, propping the phone between my chin and ear.

There are wooden steps leading down to the ocean, and even in the darkness, the waves are the prettiest crystal blue-green color. They appear almost florescent.

It's peaceful here and just so darn pretty.

"You know what?" I say at last. "I think I will stick around for a while."

"Awesome!" Noelle exclaims. "And who knows? Maybe fate will shine down on you and some hot man will show up and spice things up."

I let out a snort. "Uh, unless that groundskeeper you told me about is a secret Adonis, I don't see that happening."

Chuckling, she says, "Hmm, I think Noel mentioned he's about eighty. But you like older men, right?"

"Ugh. I like them older by a year or two, you bitch, not by fifty-seven!"

"What, wrinkly balls don't do it for you?"

I scrunch up my face and mutter, "You are so gross."

We share a laugh then, and that makes me lament, "This sucks. I'm going to miss you so much."

"I know. I'll miss you too. But that's why you have to find a way to have fun for both of us."

I assure her that I'll make the most of my time down here, no matter what.

"I promise to enjoy the sun, the sand, and the ocean—everything but wrinkly balls."

FANTASY GIRL

JAXON

Noel drops the key off for his beach house before he heads to the airport for his red-eye to Sweden.

After I tie up my own loose ends, I fly down to Florida. Two connections later find me on the island.

I have to take a jitney from the tiny regional airport to Noel's house on the beach. The island is so sparsely populated that regular taxi service isn't even an option. The driver informs me of this and that the people who work here usually return to the mainland at night.

Good, it's looking more and more like I won't be bothered by a single soul.

Noel was right. There are no Wolves fans here to worry about, and absolutely no freaking Mr. Hockeypants.

Damn, I'm still seething over that bastard and his shitty post implicating me as the primary reason for our playoff loss.

But I need to leave all that negativity behind. I'm on an island now and I cannot fucking wait to lounge on the beach and live like a hedonist.

Since there are no people to worry about, maybe I won't even bother with clothes.

"Yeah, what would be the point?" I mumble to myself after I pay the jitney driver and am jogging up to my new home. "I'm the only one around."

Once I'm inside the house—which is kickass cool, by the way—I get started on the hedonist-lifestyle by stripping down to absolutely nothing.

Man, I feel free and a little dirty, and I fucking love it.

Leaving my luggage in the entryway by the door, I pad barefoot to the kitchen.

"Sweet," I murmur upon finding it's fully stocked. "Looks like Noel's help thought of everything."

Only thing that's weird, though, is that there's a bottle of vodka on the counter. And it's open.

Hmmm, maybe the housekeeper helped herself to a nip or two before she left? Oh, well, who cares? There's plenty left.

Picking up the bottle, and flipping it ala *Cocktail*, I unscrew the cap and take a shot.

And then I take another.

Ah, hell.

I grab the whole fifth and step down into the sunken living room. That's when I spy another oddity—the sliding glass doors leading out to the patio are slightly ajar.

"Good thing robbery isn't a concern around here," I mutter to myself, shaking my head.

Dick swinging and booze in hand, I walk over to slide the doors open the whole way.

Fuck, it's gorgeous out there.

There's a beautiful private beach just down from the patio. The best part, though, is that it's all mine for as long as I want.

I can't see the entire beach area, particularly off to the left, because there's a low wall around the patio…and a bunch of flowers and crap growing wild in ceramic pots lining the top of the wall.

No worries, I can check out the whole beach area later. I think for now that I'll stay on the patio. It's close to the house for when I need to take a piss, which will be soon since I'm polishing off this fifth like a beach bum mofo.

Grabbing the edge of a chaise lounge, I drag it to a real sunny spot on the patio. A concern about my naked self crosses my mind for a hot minute. I mean, shit, what if someone *is* down on the beach, like a worker or a random passing through?

But then I realize that if I can't see anyone, no one can see me.

So yeah, I'm good.

Stretching out on the lounger, I take another shot from the bottle, while enjoying the feel of the sun warming my balls.

But wait, shit. Sunburn down there would really suck. And not in a good way.

Lucky for me, there's a big, fluffy white towel oh-so-conveniently located near my chair. When I lift it up, I uncover a bottle of sunscreen.

Wow, I'm impressed with Noel's super-thoughtful help. He told me everything would be readily available and at my fingertips, but this is taking shit to a whole new level.

I make a mental note to leave the staff an extra big tip before I leave—which, at this point, might not be for a *really* long time.

Taking advantage of the handy sunscreen, I slather it onto my legs, chest, and shoulders—*mmm, that feels good*—and then I cover my junk with the towel.

But that doesn't last long.

Sun and vodka must be good for the libido since, within minutes, I'm pitching a pretty impressive tent.

When my dick gets so hard that the towel slides off, I can't resist the call of the wild.

I bend my knees and reach down to wrap my hand around my now-throbbing cock.

"Ah, fuck, yeah," I murmur as I begin stroking.

But, man, after a minute, I realize I could use a little lube.

I stop and look around.

Hmm, that sunscreen should do. Plus—bonus!—it'll protect my dick from harmful rays.

I squirt a bunch in my hand, close my eyes, and get back to stroking. All lubed up, I start fantasizing I'm here with some hot babe.

My hand is slick enough that it's easy to pretend fantasy girl's warm mouth is on my cock.

"Yeah, suck it, baby," I groan, my hand moving faster and faster.

I pretend to flip her over so I can start drilling into her.

Fantasy girl is soon screaming, that's how damn good I am.

Shit, this is so realistic—I am fucking amazing.

But then I realize someone really *is* screaming. And it's not in ecstasy, it's in…fear?

Or is that disgust?

"Oh my God, you repulsive pervert!" a shrill female voice yells.

Hmm, we have a winner—disgust it is.

Hey, I can work with that. Though when she keeps yelling, I'm not so sure. Yappy fantasy woman is really starting to fuck with me getting off.

Sighing, I stop stroking and open my eyes.

Whoa, maybe this really is a fantasy!

Why else would the babe in front of me, though clearly furious, be hot as sin?

I look her over. Her hair is long and wild, brunette with highlights the color of new pennies. And she has a pretty face, one of those heart-shaped ones with the pert little nose.

And then there's her body, oh, her body...

She has curvy hips and big breasts that are heaving, threatening to pop out of her barely there polka dot bikini top.

Please do!

My dick demands that I keep going, so I rasp, "Can you just stand there like that for another minute, sweetheart?"

She says nothing, so I start stroking away, faster and faster.

"I'm close now," I rasp, "so fucking close—"

Fantasy girl then suddenly screams out, "Oh, no, you don't, you sick fuck!"

And before I know what's happening, a big blue planter is whizzing toward my head.

6

I THINK I JUST KILLED JAXON FREAKING HOLLAND

CARA

Oh my God—I think I just killed Jaxon freaking Holland!

That's who that is. I can see that now. Though why *he's* here on the island, not to mention at Noel's beach house, I have no idea.

But yes, it appears I have murdered a man.

How could this happen?

I run my hands through my slightly damp hair and squeak out a little, "Help."

How was I supposed to know the guy jerking off was someone other than the ancient groundskeeper? I even looked for his wrinkly balls to confirm, but unfortunately the planter was already in the air.

Of course, if I'd been able to pry my eyes away from his throbbing shaft a little sooner, I may have realized this guy is about six decades less than eighty.

And that he's Jaxon Holland.

Speaking of which, who knew he had such a giant co—

"Jesus, Cara, stop it. You just killed a man. And not just any man but a famous hockey player man."

I race over and kneel next to Jaxon's lifeless body.

Should I say a prayer or something?

I'm about to, but then I glance down.

Oh my God, his corpse is sporting wood!

Or is that the start of rigor mortis?

Hmmm...

In any case, maybe a prayer is not appropriate. Although someone really should praise God for giving this man such an impressive member.

Stop it! You're sick in the head, Cara.

Thinking shit like that when you should be preparing for your impending arrest.

Buuuutt....

I can't help but wonder what his dick would do if I touched it?

I mean, like, can dead guys come?

Oh my God, this is getting nuts.

Nuts, yeah, those look nice too. Jaxon Holland keeps his entire manly package nicely trimmed.

Or, rather, he did...till I murdered him.

Poor guy.

I shake my head and try to look anywhere but *there*.

Finally, I zone in on his face.

Ah, that's safe.

Wow, he looks so peaceful. I feel so bad. I guess I'm not only going to prison, but to hell as well.

Though prison will be hell, I'm sure.

"Why didn't you duck?" I cry out to the corpse.

And that's when the corpse's mouth twitches.

Wait, what?

I breathe a huge sigh of relief. He's not dead!

"Yes, breathe again," I urge.

I watch as he swallows.

Yay, no prison for me...and no hell either. Phew!

But we should hurry this along.

I need to ask him why he's here on the island, so I start smacking his face.

Yeah, this should help him come to. I've seen this in movies and shit.

I'm hitting him lightly, of course. I wouldn't want to wound him any further. And heaven knows I sure don't want to mar any of his stunning features.

He mumbles something incoherent then, so I stop smacking him.

Jesus, I'm so freaking glad I haven't murdered the Wolves' center. But it does appear as if I've injured him. There's an angry red welt on his temple from where the planter grazed him.

"I'm sorry," I murmur.

He needs some ice. That'll take down the swelling and help wake him up.

I jump up and hurry into the house, heading straight for the kitchen, wondering again, and this time out loud, "What is Jaxon Holland doing here?"

Noel must've invited him and not told Noelle. Ugh, just my luck that the one person I'd never want to run into—not after the mean-spirited hit piece I penned about him—is here on the island with me.

Talk about adding insult to injury! I knocked the poor guy out cold.

Sighing, I open the freezer to search for an ice pack.

Sadly, I'm out of luck. So I opt instead for a big bag of frozen carrots.

Jaxon is still coming to by the time I'm back out on the patio, but he still seems really out of it. The least I can do is make the poor man comfortable.

I scan around and spy the white towel I brought out earlier. It's lying on the ground.

I grab it up and shake it out, with dirt and flower petals from the planter I threw flying everywhere.

Once the towel looks pretty clean, I fold it over once, and then carefully place it under Jaxon's head.

His eyes are still closed as he mutters, "Mmm, thanks, Mom."

Eww!

I jump back. He thinks I'm his mom, gross. Yeesh, it didn't *seem* like I threw the planter all that hard, but maybe I did. Hopefully this is just a short-term effect, and once he fully comes to he'll be fine.

I hold the bag of carrots up to the welt on his head, while smoothing back wayward strands of sandy brown hair with my fingers...just like Mom would do.

Oh, yuck.

This disturbing train of thought must be derailed immediately. And I know of only one way to do that. It might not be pretty, but a girl's gotta do what a girl's gotta do.

Reluctantly—*oh, who the hell are we kidding? More like eagerly*—I trail my eyes down to the part of him that started this whole mess.

The offending appendage is no longer hard, but it's still mighty impressive.

I swear, though, Jaxon's dick is totally staring back at me.

And—I squint a little more closely—it's looking rather contrite.

"Hey," I whisper to his cock, "don't give me your sad, droopy one-eyed stare. You have to accept that you brought this all on yourself. If you weren't so hard and thick and..."

Whoa, where am I going with this?

I clear my throat and continue, "Anyway, if not for all of those things, I wouldn't have focused on you and only you. I would've realized who you are attached to and I wouldn't have lobbed a planter at your owner's stupid head."

Just then, Jaxon snickers.

I jump up, the bag of carrots falling to the ground with a mushy thud.

Fuck, he's awake.

And that means he heard everything.

Although, wait a second here...

I narrow my eyes.

Was he ever even out to begin with?

I'm not so sure now.

Stabbing a finger at him, I accuse, "Have you been faking being unconscious this whole time?"

He sits up, shrugging his impossibly wide shoulders as he moves the towel to cover his groin area.

Guess he doesn't trust me, seeing as I do have a strong arm and good aim.

"I don't know," he replies just as snarkily. "What do you think? Maybe I *was* awake this whole time and curious to gauge your reactions."

What?

He doesn't feel bad for duping me?

"That's just wrong!" I grind out, aghast.

"Ha," he laughs. "You're a fine one to talk about what's right and wrong. 'Wrong' is throwing heavy objects at a person's head. You could've killed me, you know?"

"Well, I didn't," I snap back. "And with what you were up to, you're lucky I didn't aim lower."

Smugly, he retorts, "I'm surprised you didn't, seeing as you seem to be quite enamored with what you saw."

"I was not!"

"Do you really expect me to believe that?" He raises a brow. "Let's review, shall we? Were you or were you not just now talking to my dick?"

I stammer, "I, uh, I-I…"

"Yeah, that's what I thought. And in my book, sweetheart, that kind of behavior means you're beyond enamored. I'd say you've moved straight into 'smitten' territory."

"You, you…"

He has me so angry that I'm seeing red. I can't even think of a good retort. He's lucky there are no other planters within my reach.

"You're disgusting," I finally spit out.

He laughs. "Offended now, are we? You're the one throwing planters and talking to my cock. If anyone has a right to be pissed, honey, it's me."

I have no defense for that, but I do feel the need to remind him, "It was *one* planter. Not multiple."

"Whatever, crazy chick."

I have to outdo him, I must! He's such a cocky— Wait, can I even 'think' that word? I heard somewhere that it was trademarked.

Anyway, where was I?

Oh, that's right, I'm schooling Jaxon Holland.

Sticking out my chest as far as I can, I declare, "For your information, I am not a 'chick.' I am a woman, mister. Learn it, live it, love it."

"Not a problem," he says, his dark green eyes sparkling with mischief as he stares at the boobs I'm pretty much sticking in his face.

"Oh, no way, buddy." Hands on my hips, I relax my shoulders and take a step back. "You know what? You are just not a gentleman."

Scoffing heartily, he proclaims, "I never claimed to be."

Ugh, why must he try to one up me on everything?

I grind out, "You're worse than 'not a gentleman.' You're a pig!" I raise my hand and tick off. "Jacking off, calling me a chick, staring at my chest—"

"This, coming from a girl who talks to a man's junk."

"So what if I do?" I shout. "Who cares if I muttered a few words to your stupid dick? He has *way* more personality than you."

"Hey now, he's not stupid," Jaxon retorts.

Of course he'd be most upset by *that* comment, as opposed to the shot at his deficit of personality.

Jesus, I have to get away from this man, along with his well-muscled body *and* that mind-muddling cock of his.

But before I go, I have one last thing to say— "At least your dick doesn't talk back!"

Chuckling, he retorts, "Oh, he's been known to spew a time or two."

I make a face. "God, you are so gross, Jaxon Holland."

As I stomp off, slamming the sliding glass doors dramatically, I hear him muttering, "Wait. How does she know who I am?"

7

DOING HER AND DUMPING HER

JAXON

How in the hell does this crazy chick know who I am?

There's only one way—she follows hockey to some extent. So much for there being no Wolves fans on the island. Just my luck.

Ah, but maybe it's not so bad. She's a hot fan, at least. I can deal with that. I'm more than up for banging a groupie, especially one that looks like her. That pretty face and that tight little body are made for sin. And I'm just the guy to do the corrupting.

Hey, she's already met my dick and she likes him. That's, like, two for two. Now we just have to bring it down the home stretch. I'll consider it a victory once I have the crazy chick underneath me, screaming out my name.

Fuck, I can only imagine what a fireball she is in bed. I'm sitting out here on the patio in the wake of her anger, and it's like she made the hot, humid air even thicker.

Hell, I could stay out here all night and bask in her leftover sexual tension, but I should probably go inside and make peace.

Not to mention, I need to get to work on bedding her.

Jiggling my now-flaccid cock, I say to him, "You and the crazy chick had a nice conversation, didn't you, bud? How about we see this thing through to the end? We need to get you inside her, eh?"

Yeah, I like to talk to my dick too. Crazy Chick doesn't get to have all the fun.

Standing, I wrap the white towel around my waist. The welt on my head is throbbing a little, but it's nothing too terrible. I think the bag of carrots helped some. I'll take them in with me so I can re-freeze them and use them again later.

I'll be fine, though. I've taken far harder hits on the ice. My body is conditioned for this kind of stuff. Plus, though I won't tell the crazy chick this, I was never really knocked out. I was play-acting to get her back and give her a little scare.

Hey, I had to fuck with her a little, hence the "mommy" comment. I chuckle now at that one.

Oh, well, at least I can say we're even now. And I forgive her for throwing the planter at me.

I realize then that I never learned her name. Crazy Chick is fitting enough but still, one should always ask for the name of their assailant. Come to think of it, I better check and make sure she's even supposed to be here.

What if she's some kind of crazy squatter?

Hmmm, well, even if she is I think I'll still fuck her before I send her on her way. She looked mighty good in that bikini. Bet she'd look even better out of it.

And with that in mind, I head inside.

Hmm, Planter Thrower isn't anywhere to be found downstairs.

Maybe that's a good thing. I don't have to worry about being brained.

I guess she retreated to an upstairs bedroom.

"Damn, I bet she nabbed the best one," I grumble.

Not that it matters, I'm not picky about my accommodations. Besides, if all goes well, we'll be sharing a bed soon enough.

After retrieving my phone from my luggage still by the door—she didn't mess with my things, so she can't be *that* crazy—I plop down on the sofa and call Noel.

It's late over in Sweden, but I catch him before he's in bed. He informs me that he just found out himself that his twin sister invited her friend to stay at his beach house.

Ah, so that's who she is.

"Yeah, I kind of met her," I say to Noel.

Hearing the sour note in my tone, he sighs. "Man, I am so sorry. If I had known, I would've warned you that someone was already there. I guess Noelle and that girl were supposed to vacation together. But my sister's plans changed at the last minute. She landed an internship for the summer after all. Since her friend was already down there, though, I guess she told her to just stay."

So she's not a squatter. Though she will be once I have her squatting on my cock.

Noel, nice guy that he is, is still busy apologizing and explaining how he left a voice mail to bring me up to speed.

I hold the phone out, and lo and behold, I do have a missed message.

"I never got it," I explain. "But I see it on here now. I was out on the patio and my phone was still inside."

"Hey, that's cool, man. It's good to know you're already putting away the electronics. Enjoy that sunshine and seclusion. That's what I always do when I'm down there. Unplug for a while."

"I intend to," I tell him since that is in my plans—along with nailing the chick with the good throwing arm, of course.

And that reminds me... "This friend of your sister's, does she have a name?"

"Yes, of course." Noel laughs. "Her name is Cara, Cara Milne. I figured since you met her that you already knew."

Met her? She caught me jacking off and threw a planter at me. So yeah, I guess you could say we're acquainted.

I decide to keep those thoughts to myself.

Instead, I simply reply, "Yeah, we met, but it was only for a minute or two. There wasn't much time for proper introductions."

I stifle a snort, since our "introduction"—if you could call it that—was far from proper.

"I see. Well, I've never met Cara, but my sister's always telling me how nice she is. I think Noelle's gearing up to introduce us since Cara doesn't have a boyfriend. But you know what? Maybe you two will hit it off."

"Cool. I'm totally up for a little island lovin'," I reply.

"Whoa, wait, slow your roll, Holland. I didn't mean *that*. Cara's a nice girl by all accounts, so don't go fucking her and breaking her heart. My sister will never let me hear the end of it if you screw over her friend."

Wow, am I really so bad?

I guess so, since doing her and dumping her is in the plan. No wonder Cara called me a pig.

I am one!

I guess Mr. Hockeypants was right too when he said I was a dog.

What's the difference, anyway?

They're both animals, right?

Suddenly, visions of stuffed squirrels and fake bongs fill my head.

Shit, no.

That's why I wanted to get away.

Fuck it, forget island lovin'. I'm never making a move on Cara Milne. Sure, I'll be cordial and friendly to her, but that's it.

I don't need the fucking hassle, nor my friend and his sister's wrath.

I've taken enough hits lately.

8

HE MUST NEVER KNOW I'M MR. HOCKEYPANTS

CARA

I retreat to my upstairs bedroom. It's quiet and serene, but damn if I can't get annoying Jaxon Holland out of my mind.

That's not good, seeing as I really, really hate the dude.

But if I hate him so much, why can't I get that hard, throbbing appendage of his to disappear from my thoughts?

It was just so long and hard and thick. I can only imagine what it'd feel like in my—

Stop!

He's a jerk...and a pig...and a dog who likes strip clubs.

Plus, he's the ditzy player who blew the big game.

Too bad that doesn't work. My traitorous body just doesn't care about those things. After seeing *all* of Jaxon Holland, I'm super worked up.

And I need a damn release!

Resigned that I'll have to take care of things myself, I peel away my pink and white polka dot bikini and pad off to the shower in the en suite bathroom.

Yep, I have some business to take care of that involves more than just washing off sand.

I locked the door when I first entered the bedroom, but I'm sure to latch the bathroom lock as well. The last thing I need is for Jaxon to walk in on me touching myself while I'm thinking of him and his impressive assets.

I wonder what **he** *was thinking about when I caught him with his hand on his dick.*

"Oh, who cares," I murmur.

For a good, long while, I just stand under the shower nozzle, relishing the feel of the warm water against my skin. The pulsating rivulets are so soothing, which is good since that damn Jaxon made me so…tense.

I turn around and the water caresses my breasts. Once I add in a dirty fantasy of Jaxon barging in and having his way with me, I am more than ready for a release.

Leaning back against the tiled wall, I enjoy the feel of the water trailing down my stomach, and then lower…to just the right spot.

"Unh…"

I have to hold onto the wall.

As warm water flows over my swollen clit, I pretend that it's Jaxon's tongue, lapping at my folds.

"Oh, that's so good, Holland. Keep doing that."

Working my way to a crescendo, I increase the water pressure…

until I am shuddering and moaning, tumbling over the edge and gasping out a somewhat garbled, "Jaxon, Jaxon."

Wait, no, stop this foolishness now.

My good sense returns the second orgasmic bliss fades. Funny how that works, huh?

Suddenly clear-headed, I realize I could never start something with Jaxon, not even an island fling. First, he's obviously very good friends with Noel Sandlund. It doesn't take a genius to figure out who invited him to the island. They're teammates, for heaven's sake. And Noelle mentioned that she hadn't spoken to her brother yet, which means he'd assume his place is empty.

For a minute, as I'm lathering a loofah to wash away the evidence of my Jaxon Holland-induced self-loving, I consider leaving the island.

But why should I do that?

I'll be damned if big-cock Holland is going to chase me away.

That's it, I'm staying!

But there's one huge caveat—Jaxon must never find out I'm Mr. Hockeypants. He'd be beyond pissed to learn he's staying with the one person who exacerbated an already bad situation for him. I'm pretty sure his leaving town and ending up here is directly related to bad fan behavior.

And who incited that firestorm?

None other than—I raise my hand—yours truly.

So yeah, no, my secret identity must remain a secret.

Yet another reason not to get involved with Jaxon. Good thing I've gotten him out of my system.

I step out of the shower and pull a towel down from the bar.

After I dry off, I slip on a pair of cute ragged-edge jean shorts, a royal blue tank top, and some strappy sandals.

Taking a deep breath, I head downstairs to face fat-cock Holland with my newfound attitude—indifference to his hotness.

CAN WE START OVER?

JAXON

I can hear the shower running when I arrive upstairs.

It's her.

Well, whatever.

I have my luggage with me and I'm just up here to choose a bedroom and unpack.

Though I was right about what I suspected earlier.

Cara—I really like her name, by the way, even though she irks the shit out of me—has chosen the master suite.

"Figures," I murmur as I pass by her closed door.

The water is still pounding away but I don't allow myself, even for a second, to imagine Cara's sexy, naked body in there, all wet and sudsed up.

Fuck, who the hell am I kidding?

That's the *only* image in my perverted mind.

"I wonder if she needs someone to soap up her back."

Don't go there, my brain says.

Hey, no, let's stop in and check, my cock counters.

It's hard to be a man sometimes.

Shaking my head, the one that does the sensible thinking, I practically run down the long hallway, away from the naked, showering Cara.

I choose the bedroom farthest away from hers to avoid temptation. That's what Cara is, by the way. She's evil temptation. She's Eve with the apple. And I'm dumb old Adam.

Oh, great, now all I can imagine is Cara curving her fingers and beckoning me to take a bite of the forbidden fruit—*her* forbidden fruit.

Fuck!

Dropping my bags, I head off to my own shower, where I need to take care of what was interrupted earlier. A good release will have me thinking clearly in no time.

And it works.

Feeling a million times better after I emerge from the shower, I dry off and throw on a pair of tan cargo shorts and a red and black Wolves' tee.

I have to admit I find it weird, though, that the water's still pounding away down the hall.

"Shit, the girl must really like to be clean," I murmur.

My stomach growls in agreement. Or maybe that's a reminder that I haven't eaten in hours. Come to think of it, I'm starving.

I head back down the hall so I can go whip up some dinner. I must be losing it, though, as I swear I hear a small moan *and* my name when I pass by Cara's door.

Nah, that can't be right.

Shit, I have to get this girl out of my head before she drives me batty.

Good thing cooking always clears my mind. I'm no master chef, mind you, but I know my way around the kitchen.

Noel promised the place would be fully stocked, and he wasn't kidding. There are thick-cut steaks, boneless chicken breasts, pre-pressed burgers, breads of all sorts, and a ton of fresh vegetables and fruits.

One thing for sure, Cara and I will be well fed for however long we're on the island.

And that has me thinking just how long she plans on staying. I should've asked Noel if he has any idea. My own plan has always been to hang around for at least a month, maybe longer. I need time for people to forget about the playoff debacle.

But now with all this good food, plus the fact I can run on the beach to stay in shape, there's absolutely no need for me to rush back to Las Vegas. I could feasibly live this island life till training camp. That is, if I really wanted to.

"And I may," I muse out loud as I toss two steaks onto the stove-top grill.

"Hey," a soft feminine voice rings out from behind me.

Startled, I twist around to find Cara standing there, seemingly much more relaxed than earlier. She also looks really cute in her cropped jean shorts and a blue tank top. Thank God she doesn't seem to be harboring any ill will toward me.

Cool, I feel the same. I'd like nothing more than to put our awkward first encounter behind us.

"Hey there," I say, not unkindly.

I also give her a friendly smile and an acknowledging nod before turning back around to resume what I was doing.

Coming up from behind me and slinking around to the side of the counter like a stealthy cat, she says softly, "How's your head? Are you feeling all right?"

"Um, yeah," I reply, confused. "I'm good."

"Oh, okay." Leaning her hip casually against the counter, she continues, "I was worried you might be suffering some kind of after-effects from the, uh, planter incident."

"Really, why's that?"

"It sounded like you were talking when I walked in."

"Oh, that." I laugh. "I was talking to myself, thinking out loud."

She cocks her head curiously as she asks, "What were you thinking about?"

I start chopping vegetables—peppers and onions—to grill along with the steaks.

"I was thinking how I may stick around on the island longer than I originally planned."

"Mmm…" Cara nods, then glances around the beautiful state-of-the-art kitchen we're in. "I can see why. Not only is the whole island gorgeous, but this house is amazing."

"Right?"

I stop chopping long enough to add, "So what about you? Do you have any idea how long you're staying?"

She hops up onto the counter, her slightly bronzed legs swinging. "Hoping to get rid of me already, huh?" she says.

Reaching over, she snatches a sliver of sweet pepper from the pile I just sliced.

Mock-swatting at her hand, I protest, "Hey, no stealing ingredients during meal prep. And to answer your question, no, I'm not looking to get rid of you. I was just curious, is all."

Nodding, she bites into the pepper.

After a minute, she says, "I don't really know how long I'm staying. Noelle and I were originally thinking a few weeks, but now I guess I'm playing it by ear."

"Wow. That sounds pretty loose and easy. Is there no job to get back to in…wait, where do you live? Vegas, I'm guessing, since you and Noelle are friends. Is that right?"

"Yes, I live in Las Vegas," she confirms.

But for some reason she seems incredibly nervous all of a sudden, even as she says, "And no, I don't have a job. I, um, inherited some money that I live off of."

I nod. "That's cool."

After I slide the veggies onto the grill, where they start sizzling along with the steaks, I hold up my hands and assure her, "Hey, there's no judgment on my part. I think it's great you have that kind of freedom."

Still looking inexplicably strained, she nods tightly and murmurs a soft, "Mmm-hmm."

Weird, maybe she has some on-the-down-low profession. Sheesh, I hope she's not a sex worker.

Or maybe I do.

No, wait, I'm not going there.

Thankfully, she interrupts my off-the-rails musings when she says, "Those steaks smell really delicious."

Cool, we can talk about dinner. That's a safe subject.

"I'm glad you think so," I say, "since one of them is for you."

She looks surprised as she asks, "Seriously?"

"Yes, of course. I wouldn't cook for myself and leave you hanging."

I get a cute smile for that. "That's sweet of you, Jaxon. I appreciate it."

I shrug. "What can I say? That's me, just your average, ordinary, sweet guy."

"Hardly ordinary." She laughs. "More like Mr. Star Hockey Player."

"Ah, that. I was wondering how you knew who I am. But now it all makes sense. Seeing as you live in Las Vegas, Cara Milne, I assume you're a Wolves fan?"

I raise a brow.

But she doesn't answer my question.

Instead, she exclaims, "Hey, how do *you* know *my* name?"

I fess up. "I called Noel while you were upstairs."

Stifling a snicker, she says, "Worried I was a psycho trespasser, huh?"

I turn the steaks and shrug. "Eh, one can never be too careful these days. Not to mention, you did throw a rather large and heavy planter at my head."

She winces. "Yeah, about that... I really am sorry. That wasn't cool."

"Don't worry about it. I'm fine." Sheepishly, I add, "I'm sorry too... for what I was doing when you walked up. I truly thought I was alone."

She turns about ten shades of red and glances away. "Can we just pretend that never happened? Maybe we can start over?"

"Sure. Let's do that right now." I wipe my hands on a towel and hold a hand out to her. "Hi, I'm Jaxon."

She takes my hand, shakes, and says, "Nice to meet you, Jaxon. I'm Cara."

Since the steaks are done, I take them off the grill, along with the peppers and onions. Then I divide everything evenly onto two plates.

"So, Cara, would you like to join me out back on the patio for a lovely dinner? We can rewrite our history out there too."

"Sure." Another blush. She's so cute. "I'd love to have dinner with you, Jaxon. And let's rewrite away."

10

I ALMOST TAKE OUT HOLLAND *AGAIN*

CARA

It's really dark out on the patio, so Jaxon lights a bunch of candles to illuminate our outdoor meal.

I watch as he does. Damn, he looks good in low light. There's a touch of sexy scruff on his strong jaw and his hair is damp and slicked back, most likely from a recent shower.

During dinner, we do what we planned—we rewrite our short but bumpy history.

And you know what? It's all good. Jaxon is nothing but sweet and courteous as we eat. He has great table manners too. Maybe I misjudged him and he's not such a pig after all.

I hope it's true, since by the time we're finished eating I'm officially having a good time.

But then, just as I'm letting my guard down, I slip back into panic mode when, out of the blue, Jaxon says, "So, you never answered my question in the kitchen. Are you a Wolves fan or not?"

Yikes, I better tread carefully.

If I reveal just how much of a rabid hockey fan I really am, Wolves fanatic in particular, it might lead to more in-depth hockey talk. I could easily slip up and reveal my secret blog identity. As evidenced by my most recent post, Mr. Hockeypants has a very specific—and not always nice—take on things.

So to play it safe, I hedge. "Um, yes, the Wolves are cool. But I don't know all that much about the team. I guess you could say that I'm not really into hockey all that much."

Ugh, my heart. It hurts to say such things about the sport I love.

But wow, I'm not the only one affected by my words. They're just about killing poor Jaxon. Like, for real killing him, no joke. He is totally choking.

So much for rewriting history, we're just repeating it here.

"Oh my God, are you all right?" I gasp, standing.

He shakes his head. He was taking a drink of water when I responded to his question. Was it really that disturbing of a reply?

I don't know, but I do know I better move my ass and save him.

I race over to his side of the little wrought iron table we're seated at and start pounding him on the back.

"Are you okay, Jaxon?"

He coughs and sputters, "I might be if you'd quit hitting me so hard."

"Oops." I drop my hand and step back. "I guess I was getting a little overzealous there, yeah?"

"You think?" Looking up at me, though with a twinkle in his green eyes, he says, "I'm beginning to think you may be a danger to my health, Miss Milne."

Hmm, does he mean because I'm always assaulting him in some way?

Or is it something else entirely?

From the dark lust swirling in his eyes, I think it may be the latter.

I go ahead and lose myself in those stormy greens, as I feel pretty much the same way. There's an undeniable chemistry between us. Too bad we can't act upon it.

Get the hell away from him, a little voice screams. *Before you do something you'll both regret.*

My conscience is right.

Stumbling over to my side of the table, I sit down with a thud. But because I'm all discombobulated now, I begin to ramble.

"I really am sorry, Jaxon. I'm sorry to pound on your back like that. I just didn't want you to choke to death. I mean, where's the closest hospital even? I think over on the mainland. We'd probably have to medevac you out of here."

He chuckles and agrees, "Yes, probably. So thank you for helping me to avoid an embarrassing situation like that."

"Hmm, maybe it's not me that's a danger to your health." I glance around to where we are. "Maybe we just need to stay off this patio from now on."

I'm totally joking, but he plays along, nodding thoughtfully. "It does already seem to be the scene of many crimes."

"Right?" I agree. "And to think, this is only our first day."

"Heaven help us," he says, raking his hand through his hair.

I try not to think about how one of the many crimes involved me catching him with that very same hand wrapped around his cock.

Oh, how I wish he'd be a repeat offender on that one.

"Yeah, that was hot," I murmur on a sigh.

"What was hot?" he asks.

Wonderful, he just has to have great hearing too.

"Uh, um," I stammer, pointing down to the tiny bit of steak left on my plate. "I was just thinking how the food was really hot, which is, uh, good since no one wants cold steak."

God, kill me now. I'm embarrassing myself.

A smile plays at Jaxon's lips. He obviously knows I'm not talking about the steak, but he lets it slide.

"Well, I'm glad it was hot," he says. "And since there's hardly any left, I'm guessing it means you liked it."

"Liked it? I loved it," I exclaim.

That gets us back on track, and we talk a few minutes about dinner.

But then I decide to ask, "So, Jaxon, you obviously live in Vegas now, but where do you hail from?"

He chuckles. "I guarantee you've never heard of the place."

"Try me," I say.

That earns me a raised brow, but I don't care. Shut up, a little harmless flirtation won't hurt anyone.

Smiling, he says, "I'm from Thunder Bay, Ontario."

I shiver even though it must be eighty degrees. "Yikes, that even sounds cold," I murmur.

"It is cold," he confirms. "The winters are brutal. But it makes for lots of great frozen ponds to skate on and play hockey on. That was my life while I was growing up."

"That sounds fun." I lean back in my chair and wave toward the moonlit sandy beach, where the waves are hitting the shore in rhythmic crashes. "So which do you prefer?" I ask. "Do you like it hot or cold?"

He thinks about it. "Well, I'll always love home because, well, it's home. But this is much nicer weather-wise. So I guess when it comes to climate, I prefer hot."

I agree. "This is rather perfect."

An island breeze blows just then, making all the candles flicker.

"Hey," Jaxon says, "I have an idea. Would you want to take a walk down on the beach? It's such a beautiful night, and I bet the surf rolling in is really warm."

Hmm, do I want to take a stroll on a moonlit beach with a gorgeous, hot hockey player?

"Hell yeah," I blurt out, way more enthusiastically than necessary.

"Okay, then." Jaxon chuckles. Standing, he sweeps his hand out in front of him. "Ladies first."

I kick off my sandals and walk down the wooden steps into the cool sand.

Jaxon follows, ditching his beat-up Chucks before joining me.

"This is nice," he says as we begin walking down to the water.

And you know what? It really is.

I just hope it stays this way.

GIVE ME BACK MY EFFING BALLS

JAXON

Surprisingly, as the days go by, Cara and I get along exceedingly well. Guess rewriting our history is working out. There are no more near-death experiences, and we just enjoy island life. We even fall into a bit of a routine—hanging out on the beach during the day, sharing meals together all the time, and taking long walks on the beach every single night.

I really like those walks the best, but I don't tell Cara. I don't want to give her the wrong impression.

Strolling under the moonlight, the waves lapping at our feet, could easily be construed as something romantic.

And that could lead to her thinking we're a burgeoning couple.

Perish the thought!

We most definitely are not. We are simply friends, nothing more. I mean, I barely even beat off to her anymore.

Okay, that's a lie. I do all the time. But keeping shit platonic between us outside of fantasy life is rule number one. There isn't now, nor will there ever be, anything but good ole friendship between me and Cara Milne.

We haven't discussed it or anything, it's just understood. I think that's why we don't do anything stupid, like hold hands or become overly touchy.

Man, though, there are times I'd like to, like tonight.

We've been walking along the beach for a while now this beautiful evening, and I've been sneaking in surreptitious glances over at Cara every chance I get.

Why does she have to look so damn pretty tonight?

Her long auburn hair is blowing in the warm breeze and that sexy dress she has on is killing me. The flimsy thing's all flowy and shit, like it's made of gauze. I swear it's practically see-through.

Hey, that gives me an idea…

It's mischievous and she might call me out on it, but what the hell.

As soon as the next wave crashes in, I kneel down and skim my hand through the foamy surf.

"Mmm, the water's so nice and warm tonight," I murmur.

Cara rolls her eyes and shakes her head. "It's *always* nice and warm, Jaxon."

"Oh"—I raise a brow—"is that right, Miss Know-it-All. In that case, I guess you won't mind a little"—I toss a big scoop of water at her, aiming for her breasts—"splash."

Score! I hit those babies perfectly.

Cara jumps back, exclaiming, "Jaxon! I can't believe you just did that."

Shit, I did. And that gauzy material is totally fucking transparent when wet.

Fuck me, Cara's not wearing a bra, either. Her dark nipples, puckered and pert, stick to the material so completely that she may as well be nude up top.

I suddenly want nothing more than to peel away that dress and do very bad things to her.

But I must control myself.

Voice raspy with lust, I retort, "Believe it, baby."

Playfully, I flick more water at her, this time aiming lower, making her warn, "That's it, Jaxon. I'm done playing."

"Ooh." I pretend to shake. "I'm so scared."

Bending down, she scoops up a handful of ocean water and tosses it at my head.

I duck, but end up soaked.

"There!" she smugly declares. "I got you back."

With water dripping down my face, I point at her and declare, "This is war, baby."

"Bring it on, Jaxon."

"Oh, I intend to."

Another wave rolls in and this time I drag Cara out into it.

"No fair!" she yells.

"Who ever said war is fair?" I volley back as I dunk her head under water.

She comes up sputtering and spitting mad. Using her whole arm, she pushes another incoming wave right into me.

With both of us now sopping wet, we laugh and drop to our knees in the surf. We then splash each other till we're beyond soaked. My cargo shorts and white tee are plastered to me, and her dress... Well, let's just say she may as well not be wearing anything at all.

When we stop to catch our breath, she sees me staring.

Crossing her arms over her breasts, she questions, "Jaxon?"

This is so out of our carefully constructed friend zone.

I look away and mumble, "Sorry."

Slowly, she lowers her arms. "No, it's okay."

Shit, she's saying *look at me*, so I do.

The gauzy material is sticking to her lithe form like a body suit, accentuating the sexy swell of her hips, the inviting curve of her breasts, and the fact that it looks like she shaves *every*where.

Kill me now.

"Cara," I say roughly, "what are we doing?"

"Uh…" She peers out into the ocean and whispers, "I don't really know."

I blow out a breath and scrub my hand down my face. "Do you think this is a good idea?"

Wrong thing to say, I just killed the mood. Her eyes snap to me, hurt.

I am such an ass.

Sighing, she mutters, "I should head back to the house so I can get inside and dry off."

Fix it, fix this now.

But I don't.

I just murmur a flat, "Okay."

A part of me doesn't want to go in. A part of me would like to stay out here and let things unfold. But I know where that would go and it'd be stupid. I just got caught up in the moment for a second there. And she did too. But it's over now.

Standing abruptly, I offer her a hand. "You ready to go back?"

She ignores my hand, and scoffing, stands on her own. "Yeah, let's just get out of here, Jaxon," she snaps.

A wall is erected, and we walk back to the house in complete silence.

The whole next day, we avoid each other.

She finishes with breakfast long before I even make my way downstairs. And then, when I'm readying to start down to the beach, she lingers up on the patio.

"Are you coming down to the water?" I ask.

Dragging her chair over to a shady spot, she says, "No, I think I'm going to stay up here today." She holds up her tablet. "I'd like to get in some reading."

Guess that's my cue not to offer to join her.

That night, we skip our usual walk on the beach.

I start to worry that I've really fucked things up, but by the next day shit seems to return to normal.

I'm glad about that, but I'm also more resolute than ever that we not get involved. This bump in the road has been a good reminder not to let lust or emotions take over…ever.

That's good; we can simply go back to the friend zone.

Or can we?

When we resume our nightly walk that evening, Cara is wearing another sexy-ass dress. And, again, I can't keep my damn eyes off of her.

Does she choose these clothes on purpose?

This one is a light cotton number with tiny pearl buttons running all the way down the front. It's very sexy, very inviting.

Shit.

Can't she just wear long shorts and a T-shirt like I do?

It's like she's dressing this way to taunt me. But that can't be right. She wouldn't do that after my rejection the other night. Plus, let's be honest, she could wear a burlap sack and I'd still want her.

Guess Mr. Hockeypants was right all along—I am a dog.

So, *woof*, let the panting begin.

It's hot tonight, humid too. No surprise then that, as we're walking, Cara undoes the top buttons on her dress.

"It's really muggy out, huh?" she says.

I clear my throat and avert my gaze from the sexy swell of her tan breasts.

"It sure is," I murmur.

Despite my attempts to look at anything but her, my eyes keep tracking back. How could they not? Cara's such a beautiful, sexy woman. It's all I can do to keep my hands to myself, even. Fuck the other night, I want to touch, squeeze, and lick every delicious inch of her body.

Whoa, wait!

Not this again. This is getting out of hand.

Based on how the other night ended, and the next day of silent treatment, I bet Cara would kick my ass if I were to make a move now.

Though there aren't any planters around, so I might be safe.

Then I remember Noel's warning—don't fuck around with his sister's friend unless it's for real. Though I've grown to genuinely care for Cara, a relationship is the last thing I need or want. I mean, shit, that'd totally screw with my strip club outings. Not that I've gone to any lately. But I could feasibly take a boat over to the mainland and hit up one. Florida does have some of the best girls in the biz, after all.

Still, for some weird, unknown reason, I don't have the urge to do that.

Ah, but I like knowing I have the option.

So yeah, no—there'll be no making a move on Cara.

But damn if the urge to do exactly that isn't going away. It's getting fucking stronger.

Touch her, reach out and trail your hand down her arm. Grab her hand, or better yet, wrap her up in your arms and kiss her like you mean it.

No!

Help. Mayday, mayday.

I rack my brain for an innocuous topic to distract me from Cara's body and her luscious lips. Problem is she and I have covered most of the basic things. I know all sorts of stuff about her, thanks to these nightly walks. I know where she lives in Las Vegas—which, as fate would have it, isn't far from my own home—and I know lots of other things too.

Like that...her favorite color is purple.

Her favorite food is steak.

She likes indie music but hates speed metal.

"Yeah, I'm with you on that one," I agreed when she divulged that fact.

She also despises pickles with a passion.

I've told her lots of things about me too. Like that I don't really have a favorite color, but I think teal is pretty cool. It reminds me of the beach.

I also shared with her that I'm a hardcore classic rock fan.

Not big on pickles either, especially those disgusting chip ones. *Ugh.*

Oh, but I'm with her on the awesomeness of steak.

Suddenly, that gives me an idea—I'll bring up steak since food talk is always safe talk.

Yeah, that'll get my brain back on track.

I clear my throat, then mention to her how fortuitous it was that I made steak our first night.

She nods and agrees, "Yes, Jaxon, it really was the perfect choice for our first dinner together."

"It really was, wasn't it?" I reply smugly.

"Ooh, someone's feeling cocky tonight," she teases.

I square up my shoulders and say, "I prefer to call it confidence, honey."

"Honey, huh?"

I just love taunting her. If I can't kiss her, the next best thing is teasing the crap out of her.

I smirk over at her, and she leans in just enough to elbow me in the side.

"Oomph," I pretend to grunt.

"Aw, poor baby," she mocks.

I give her a look. "Seriously, woman, I know you're not big on hockey, but have you ever considered playing? There are women leagues out there, you know? And they could use someone like you, doling out mean-ass checks like that one."

I pretend to rub my side, and she laughs.

"No, I've never considered playing hockey, Jaxon. I'm not that good of a skater."

"Aww…" I make a sad face. "That's too bad."

Suddenly looking thoughtful, what with tapping her chin and all, she says, "That wasn't really a 'check' anyway. It was more of an elbow. And, as you well know, I'd get called for a penalty if I did something like that on the ice."

Hmm, for someone who purports to know little to nothing about hockey, she sure is well-versed on penalty calls. Just the other day, when we were lying out on the beach, two little lizards were playing in the sand. When one took out the other by knocking his legs out from under him, Cara exclaimed, "Hey, that big lizard just totally slew footed his little buddy."

"Slew footed, eh?" I squinted over at her. "Been brushing up on our hockey penalty calls lately, have we?"

"Nah," she replied, blushing inexplicably. "I just heard that term once during a game."

Yeah, right, like it's called so often.

Glancing over now, I raise a brow. "Are you sure you don't secretly follow hockey, Cara?"

Why the hell does she suddenly look so uneasy?

"Um, no, I told you I don't," she replies. "But it's not like I've never seen a game."

I'm not letting her off the hook, not tonight, not like I did the other day with the lizard. I dropped that slew foot remark way too easily. I'm getting to the bottom of this now.

Clearing my throat, I counter, "You know, most people don't pick up on all the penalty calls for a *long* time. It's funny how you seem to know even the seldom-called ones."

She shrugs. "What can I say? Maybe I'm a quick learner and retain knowledge well?"

"Is that a question?" I say.

"Um, no, that's my explanation."

"Hmm, is it now?"

I'm still wary, especially when she blurts out, "Enough with the hockey talk."

Oh, I bet she wants to change the subject.

Since I always seem to let her get her way, though, I, of course, relent. "Okay."

"So…" She blows out a breath, looking much more comfortable. "Did I tell you I heard from Noelle the other day?"

"No."

"Well, I did. And she's been really busy with her new internship. Good thing she loves it so much, right?"

Ah hell, from hockey talk to girly talk. I care about Noelle's internship about as much as I care for pickle chips. And we all know how I feel about them.

That's why I don't know why in the hell I blow out a long, capitulating breath. But I do. I go along with the subject change.

I swear this girl has me by the balls, and she's not even my girlfriend. Hell, we aren't even fuck buddies.

Yeah, so what is going on?

"She likes it, eh?" I reply flatly. "That's awesome."

I barely know Noelle. I've met her a few times when she was with Noel, and that's it. Still, I listen to every single one of Cara's updates about the girl. It's like I've turned into a desperate puppy dog, hanging on to this woman's every word like she's my whole world.

But she's not.

So what the fuck is happening here?

Shit, I know what's happening—I'm starting to like Cara way more than a bud. I like her, and I obviously lust over her.

Hmm, I see impending disaster, a disaster known as "falling in love." Isn't that what comes next in these situations?

Well, sorry, but I don't do "love."

Spinning around with no warning, I interrupt Cara. "Hey, not to cut you off, but I think we should head back to the house."

"Why?" She bites her lip, naturally confused. "We've only walked a short distance, Jaxon. We usually go much farther than this."

"Yeah, I know, but…I just thought of something I need to do."

"Like what?" she presses.

"It's personal," I snap.

"Um, okay, cranky, let's start back then."

The lost and forlorn expression on Cara's pretty face as we walk to the house pains me. But I don't say or do anything to explain my sudden change in behavior.

We just continue in silence to the light, glowing like a homing beacon, that we left on in the living room.

Like the other night, part of me wants to stop and say, "Fuck it, let's turn back around and keep going. Let's see where moving forward takes us."

But I do no such thing. I need to stay strong on this. All these walks on the beach, sharing dinners, spending days together, getting to know one another, it's just too much.

I need to backtrack, in more ways than one, and retrieve what I've so clearly lost—my fucking balls.

12

MEN ARE SO WEIRD

CARA

Men are so weird. Now I remember why I don't date all that much.

Not that I'm dating Jaxon—hush your mouth!—but even friendship with the opposite sex can be confusing.

It must be that pesky Y chromosome they possess—not only does it give them a dick, but it tends to turn them into one from time to time.

Like now.

Color me confused, but I thought Jaxon and I were having a nice time walking on the beach. We had a weird day yesterday, sure, after he was staring at my boobs through my wet dress the night before, which I'm still not sure what to make of.

But still, I thought we were past that.

Guess not.

Why else would he want to go back to the house so badly all of a sudden?

Personal reasons, my ass.

I don't bother pressing him any further, though. He made it clear he doesn't want to talk about it.

I shoot a sidelong glance his way.

Look at him over there, strutting back to the house in silence. Jerk.

By the time we reach the back patio, the tension is thick. Mr. Gruff and Grumpy heads straight indoors, muttering something about... balls?

There's no way I heard that right.

No matter, I have some muttering of my own to do.

Like when I say, "Good, go. Take your Y chromosome with you."

Too bad Jaxon's already inside and doesn't hear me.

Maybe this is all for the best, though. A little space could do us some good. Things have been confusing as hell lately. Some days it feels like we're building...a relationship?

Ugh, that can't happen.

We're far too comfortable with each other already. And that's not good. What if he finds out I'm Mr. Hockeypants?

Bet he won't be staring at my boobs then. Or maybe he will, but only because he'd want to hate-fuck me.

I don't want that. Angry fuck, yes. Hate fuck, no. It would hurt too much when he got up and left me. And leave me is what he'd do if he knew the truth.

So I need to be more careful.

I slipped up a few times when I forgot that I'm supposed to be clueless about hockey. I'm bound to end up busted for real if this crap continues.

Fuck it, my Mr. Hockeypants blog comes first. That's my job, goddammit!

Speaking of which, it's been a while since I posted anything. Last was the one I now secretly call "The Skewering of Jaxon Holland."

Though with the way he acted tonight, I don't feel so bad right now. *Ack, maybe I do a little.*

No matter, I need to focus on putting up a blog post tonight. The Stanley Cup championship is well underway, we're two games in. The Oilers are playing the Devils, and the series is tied 1-1.

There are no TVs in the house, but there is Wi-Fi. That's how I've been keeping up with things. I watched the first two games secretly in my bedroom on my tablet.

I'm pretty sure I heard Jaxon watching Game Two as well, down the hall. He was screaming something about bad officiating. No surprise there. Ever since that fateful hooking call on him, he thinks each and every infraction should be dealt with.

Not that I blame him. That penalty still haunts the poor man.

I suddenly feel a pang of guilt for egging on that hysteria.

"I won't do that again," I murmur to myself as I head inside.

After I freshen up a little in the downstairs powder room, I settle in on the sofa with my tablet, all prepared to compose a new post.

As I type it up, I'm cognizant not to mention Jaxon, or even the Wolves, in my Mr. Hockeypants's musings.

Nope, I discuss only the teams who are playing for the Stanley Cup, nothing else.

When I hit Publish, I do so with a smile. It actually feels good to post something positive. Damn, I'm kind of proud I wrote two full pages of material and didn't bash a single player. Mr. Hockeypants must be turning over a new leaf.

But it doesn't matter. Not ten seconds later, the negative comments start rolling in.

It's a slow trickle at first. The fans simply start bitching about various plays in the most recent games. But it escalates quickly into a crescendo of anti-Jaxon comments.

"No, no, no," I gasp as I helplessly watch the vitriol roll in. "How is this even happening? I never mentioned Jaxon, not even once."

I can't unpublish the post, and I can't turn off the comments. Either might make things worse, like adding chum to already bloodied waters. The haters would just migrate to other blogs and bitch even more, anyway.

No, it's better to keep this contained to one site—mine.

So I do nothing.

I sit, watching in horror as the masses once again descend on and tear apart Jaxon Holland.

In my heart, I know he'll end up discovering who's behind Mr. Hockeypants. I just feel it in my bones. And when he does, he's going to hate me so freaking much.

Now why does that make me want to cry?

MR. HOCKEYPANTS KILLS MY BONER

JAXON

That goddamn fucking Mr. Hockeypants!

I just checked my phone for a quick Stanley Cup update and what do I find? My nemesis has posted something on his sleazy blog.

He made no mention of me, thank Christ, but it doesn't matter. My haters haven't forgotten his previous post. You know the one, the post that ruined my life.

"Jesus, don't these people have anything better to do?" I grumble as I scroll through the comment thread, where meanness flows like a dirty river.

The Wolves need to trade Jaxon Holland.

Yeah, he sucks.

I hope he chokes next time he eats an edible.

The Wolves could be playing for the Stanley Cup right now if it weren't for Hotbox Holland.

Hotbox Holland?

I have to look that one up. When I discover it's another reference to getting high, I just about scream.

Thanks a lot for sullying my reputation, Mr. Hockeypants. Everyone in the world thinks I'm a stoner who gets high before the games. No one cares what players do on their own time, but toking up at game time is just unprofessional.

Great, just great. I am so pissed. Maybe I can sue Mr. Hockeypants and shut his tawdry blog down for good.

Ooh, the justice that would be served if that were to happen.

Revenge is sweet and best served cold. Good thing I'm an iceman, in more ways than one, which sort of fits with the whole hockey connection.

This is perfect and just what I need to feel better—planning my vengeance.

Wow, I came back to the house to retrieve my balls, and I have fucking found them. Plus, bonus! Not only are my balls back in my possession, they're bigger than ever.

I knew backing off from Cara was the right move.

Dropping my phone onto the bed, I remove my shirt and puff out my chest. My shorts hang low on my waist as I stand in front of the mirror on the back of the door.

Shit, I'm pretty strong and ripped, but all fired up like this I look formidable.

Good. I'm a man. I need to remember that.

"And this man needs a beer," I announce, feeling all über-male.

Tromping down the steps like a charging boar, I grunt to Cara,

"Hey."

She's on the sofa, rushing to darken her tablet for some unknown reason.

"Trying to hide your porn?" I snicker.

"You wish," she banters back.

Yeah, honey, I kind of do.

When I reach the base of the staircase, I straight-up ask, "What's so secretive, anyway?"

"None of your business," she snaps.

Her dismissive, bitchy tone irks me, so I growl, "Thought you were into sharing, Miss"—my voice goes up an octave to mimic her—"I-hate-pickles-and-just-*love*-indie- music."

Her eyes jump to me. There's hurt in her hazels. "What's gotten into you, Jaxon?"

I resist the urge to pound my chest, à la Tarzan, as I smugly retort, "Testosterone, baby. Pure male testosterone."

"Hmm, and here I thought steroids were illegal."

"Ha-ha, smartass."

Snarky Cara is back and in full swing. Good. Jaxon with his balls intact likes it when we're sparring.

Folding my arms over my chest, a move I know makes me look even stronger but is a little less obnoxious than the Tarzan chest-beating thing, I inform her, "For the record, I don't need steroids. I have plenty of testosterone to spare, sweetheart."

"Well then, maybe you should go back upstairs and 'spare' a little. We all know how good you are at *that*."

I laugh. The cojones on this girl, I love it!

Raising a brow, I ask, "Are you referring to when you caught me jacking off? *That's* your best insult?"

"Hmm, maybe it is. And maybe it does bother you a little."

"Not a chance. Like I care," I scoff. "In fact, you're welcome to watch me any time I touch myself. You just let me know and we'll make it happen."

Shit, for a second there she looks…intrigued?

Fuck…

My dick twinges.

But she schools her features to neutral and bites out, "You're disgusting."

"Oh, really?" I smirk knowingly. "You sure didn't look disgusted three seconds ago. I think you were actually contemplating taking me up on my very generous offer."

That sends her into fuming territory.

Jumping up, she tosses her tablet onto the sofa and stomps over to me.

"You know what, Jaxon Holland? You can just go fuck yourself."

I meet her toe-to-toe, staring intently into her fiery green-brown eyes. "Is that an invitation, Cara Milne? You still want to watch, or would you like to help this time?"

"That is *never* going to happen," she murmurs as she looks away.

Cupping her chin, making her meet my gaze, I utter a soft, "Are you sure about that?"

Licking her lips, she stares at my mouth.

Damn, I think she wants me to kiss her, like seriously.

Oh, what the hell, my testosterone-driven self says inside my head.

I lean in tentatively, in case I'm reading this wrong and she starts smacking the crap out of me.

But when no hits come—just her soft, warm breaths comingling with mine—I keep going.

Before our lips meet, though, I give her one last chance to back out.

"Tell me to stop, Cara," I murmur.

"No," she sighs.

I pull back an inch. "Wait, is that 'no, stop'…or 'no, don't stop'?"

"Damn it, Jaxon." She grabs my shoulders and yanks me to her.

Whoa, Cara has surprising strength for such a tiny thing.

She yanks me again, and there's no more doubt. She really wants this to happen.

So I quit resisting and just fucking kiss the girl.

And what a kiss it is.

Our lips are engaged in a stormy crash, like the waves on the beach. She cants one way and I the other, and our tongues tangle in a battle for dominance, like everything is with us.

She bites me at one point, and I yank back her hair.

"Bad girl," I tell her.

"So punish me, Jaxon."

Fuck.

My mouth returns to hers with a vengeance as I back her toward the sofa. All the while my hands are plying at her soft ass through the thin material of her dress. But, fuck, I want to feel her skin. So I reach down and hike up the damn material.

I can't wait to get this thing off of her.

When I discover she's wearing a thong, I groan and palm her bare ass.

Her hands fist in my hair, yanking and pulling.

Ow, fuck, but so damn hot.

I lay her back on the sofa, settling in between her legs. We continue kissing like that for awhile, but then we add in some pumping and grinding.

As I thrust against her soaking-wet panties—*fuck*—she shifts so that the bulge in my shorts rubs over her clit again and again—*double fuck*.

I lift my weight up off her so I can undo the rest of those pearly buttons on her dress. Her chest heaves as she watches me. Fuck, we're both breathing so hard. It's like we're wild animals preparing to rut. It's definitely primal and raw between us, and I like it.

But just as I'm peeling back the top of her dress, exposing her pebbled nipples, the tablet pops out from beneath us and clatters to the floor.

And then it flashes on.

I look down, muttering, "What the fuck?"

I see now what she was trying to hide. And let me tell you, it's an instant mood killer.

"*You're* a Mr. Hockeypants fan?" I sit up like I've just been doused with a bucket of ice water. It feels like I have.

"I can't believe you read that garbage," I go on. "You said over and over that you don't even like hockey."

"I, uh, I didn't say I hated it."

She sits up next to me, messily buttoning her dress.

I sense she's stalling, so I press, "Well, do you or don't you follow that fuckhead's blog?"

God, her face is so flushed. She's beyond flustered.

Is it because she's embarrassed over reading Mr. Hockeypants, or is it a leftover response from being aroused?

Shit, I can't tell.

But I can tell you one thing—I want some damn answers.

14

CHOOSING MY WORDS CAREFULLY

CARA

Jaxon asks again if I'm a fan of Mr. Hockeypants.

What do I say? This is like my worst nightmare come true.

I should've written the post in my bedroom, or at least turned off the tablet instead of hitting Sleep.

Now I have to explain myself, and no matter which way I go, I'm fucked. If I tell Jaxon *I'm* Mr. Hockeypants, it's over between us, as friends or as anything else.

And after making out with him on the sofa just now, which was totally hot, I'd really like to explore that "anything else" option.

But I also hate to blatantly lie to him.

I know what I'll do—I'll explain fully. I'll just need to choose my words wisely.

"Uh, I don't follow that blog," I state.

Totally true since I don't follow it, I *write* the damn thing.

Jaxon frowns. "Okay, so why'd it pop up like that? It had to have been the last thing you were looking at before I came downstairs."

"It was, yes." I nod.

See, more truth. I'm two for two here.

"And…" He waves his hand around to move me along. "Why were you reading a hockey blog when you don't like hockey? And why would you try to hide it from me?"

Oh, shit. Both are good questions, but I think I'm okay. Jaxon just gave me an idea.

Taking a deep breath, and making sure my boobs remain secured since I did such a half-assed job re-buttoning my dress, I begin to spin a tale that's sure to bite me in the ass down the road.

"Well, first," I begin, "I've been checking out hockey boards and various blogs lately because… Well, because *you* play hockey."

That scores me a point. Jaxon's smiling big and wide as he asks, "Is that right?"

"Yes." I nod, feeling pleased this is going so well. "I hid what I was looking at because I noticed Mr. Hockeypants has written some, uh, less than flattering things about you recently."

"That's an understatement," he grumbles.

I clear my throat. "Anyway, I didn't want you to see that and have your feelings hurt all over again."

"Have my feelings hurt all over again?" He laughs. "Don't worry, Cara. I'm a big boy. I can take the heat. Still, that doesn't mean the prick who wrote that crap doesn't deserve a beatdown."

Eek!

I squeak out, "He seems a little harsh at times, but I'm sure that's just his shtick."

"His shtick, eh?" Jaxon scoffs. "Well, he can take his shtick and shove it up his ass. Or better yet, I'll shove it there for him. Dude fucked up my whole world. Why do you think I came down to the island in the first place?"

"Um…"

Can I just slink away in shame now?

Jaxon jumps up and starts pacing. "I'll tell you why, Cara. I came here to hide. I had fans sending me stuffed squirrels and fucking fake bongs! I had people heckling me whenever I went out, and fans screaming rude things in my face."

God, I didn't know it was so bad. I wish I'd never written that stupid post about him. That's it. As soon as I'm alone, I'll delete it. Sure, the post will always be out there in cyberspace somewhere, but at least no one visiting the blog will happen upon it.

"I didn't know," I whisper, lowering my face to my hands. "I am so sorry, Jaxon."

He sits next to me, draping his arm over my shoulders. "S'okay, Cara. It's not like it's your fault."

But it is, I almost confess. *It so fucking is!*

I can't say that, though. I'm afraid to come clean. I mean, damn, he wants to beatdown Mr. Hockeypants and shove stuff up his ass. *Yikes.*

I realize then that no matter how badly I want Jaxon Holland, I was right all along—he and I can never be.

15

IT'S OVER BEFORE IT EVER EVEN BEGAN

JAXON

Cara starts crying, like full-on sobbing.

What the actual fuck?

I thought I was feeling bad about Mr. Hockeypants. Seems the dude has the power to upset anyone who reads his wicked words, even someone who barely understands hockey.

I try to comfort her.

"Hey, hey, it's all right. Everything will be okay." With my arm still draped around her, I pull her closer to me.

Hmm, we're such a nice fit. It's going to be so good when we finally fuck.

Suddenly, though, something dawns on me—maybe she's crying because of what we were doing before the tablet dropped to the floor. Does she regret making out with me, kind of like buyer's remorse?

Or maybe she just doesn't want me anymore after reading Mr. Hockeypants's blog.

His damn trash talk, so many outright lies. How could she know for certain I'm not some secret stoner who tokes up before big games, or that I'm not solely responsible for our shortened playoff run?

It takes a whole team to win, though. Maybe I should explain that to her since she's not fully up on hockey.

So I do just that—I pour out my thoughts, including that I'm not the man Mr. Hockeypants portrays me to be.

"I'm not that awful, I swear," I insist.

"I know that," she cries.

Then why's she still so upset?

I suddenly remember the one thing Mr. Hockeypants wrote that *was* true. That has to be what's weighing on her, especially after what we were just doing.

"Uh, Cara," I say quietly. "Are you crying because of what Mr. Hockeypants said about me going to strip clubs?"

She doesn't reply, so I continue, "It's true that I have gone to a few in the past. Er, well, okay maybe more than a few. But I swear that I haven't been to one in over a month. And I could go too, even here on the island. Well, not on the island itself, but I could take a boat over to the mainland and find a club."

She scrunches her face in disgust. "Ugh, Jaxon, are you for real right now?"

I hasten to add, "I'm not saying I would do that. I'm just making a point. I could go to those places if they were still important to me."

She blinks up at me. "You're saying they're not?"

I shake my head emphatically. "No, not anymore."

Maybe I'm maturing, or maybe Cara really has a hold on me,

seeing as the next words out of my mouth are, "I can honestly swear to you, Cara, that if we ever did become more than friends, I would never step foot in any strip club ever—"

Whoa, suddenly she starts crying harder than ever.

Fuck, I can't do anything right.

I give up and just hold her. She clings to me like this might be the last time we're ever this close physically.

But that can't be right. With the way we were all over each other just minutes ago, there's no way we're not continuing where we left off.

And fuck Noel, I'm going for it.

While we're at it, fuck me too.

I was pussying out when we were out on the beach earlier this evening, but no more. I'm ready to man up. Maybe this will end up being nothing more than an island fling, who knows? And maybe Noel and his sister will hate me forever. But I'll take that chance, as long as Cara's okay with it. Because this could also be the start of something more than a fling, and I'm finally ready. I'm not going to run. I like Cara, I like her a lot. And we have off-the-charts chemistry. So I'm done wimping out. It's time to admit I could see myself dating her. I could even see myself in a relationship with her.

And that, my friends, is stunning.

Does this mean I'm evolving?

Who knows?

All I do know is that I want to try.

But I better check with Cara first, to make sure we're on the same page.

"Cara, I need to ask you something," I say in my most serious tone.

Peering up at me, tears still welling in her eyes for some unknown reason, she nods for me to go on. "Okay."

I let go of her so I can lean back against the cushions. This is serious stuff here.

"So, about what happened earlier with us, I need to ask you—"

She holds up her hand and starts shaking her head. "Just forget it ever happened, Jaxon. Okay?"

"Huh?" I'm boggled.

"I'm sorry," she goes on. "I lost control. And that was stupid of me. In any case, I promise it'll never happen again."

"Wait, what? Where's this coming from?"

16

I JUST EFFED MYSELF

CARA

Poor Jaxon, he looks so confused. And why wouldn't he be? He has no idea we can never be because I'm his biggest nemesis on the planet.

It just would never work.

Oh, the troubles we bring onto ourselves.

I should never have kissed him.

"Cara, seriously, I need you to talk to me. Tell me what the hell is going on. Did I do something wrong?"

"No," I choke out as I scoot over to the far end of the sofa.

I need the distance to stay strong. If I remain seated next to a half-naked Jaxon, the lure of his potent male pheromones could lead to weakness on my part. Guess he does have testosterone to spare. Must be why I keep having the urge to grab his face and kiss the crap out of him, even when I know I can't.

Jaxon seeing the blog has woken me up. I was being irrational before, forgetting about reality.

God, this so totally sucks. I just want to run upstairs and lock myself in my bedroom.

But Jaxon asked for an explanation, and I should give him one. He deserves at least that.

It can't be the truth, though. Imagine me saying, "Oh, hey, bet you didn't know you were just rolling around and sucking face with Mr. Hockeypants. He doesn't have a dick, but he's pretty good at fucking you, right?"

Yeah, I doubt that would go over well.

So on to plan B.

I clear my throat and get started.

"Um, I think we just got caught up in the moment, Jaxon. But we shouldn't go there. I mean, think about it. Before we started kissing, we were ready to kill one another."

Jaxon snorts, "I think that's called foreplay, sweetheart."

He looks directly at me then, and help me, sweet baby Jesus, the smolder in his eyes almost breaks me. Good thing I'm down on the other end of the sofa where I can gather myself.

Still, I stand so I can put more space between us.

"Jaxon…"

"Yes, Cara?"

Wringing my hands, I say, "Don't you get it? This isn't something that can happen. It would never work out with us."

"Why not?" he wants to know.

Ugh, he's making this so hard, sitting there with his muscular, tan arms crossed over his smooth, wide chest.

He is so freaking hot.

Why can't this happen again?

Oh, yeah, because I doubt he wants to fuck Mr. Hockeypants. Fuck him over, yeah. But be with him as close as two people can get, probably not.

But he's not buying this vague talk. I'm going to have to go full-bitch on him. This is going to suck, because from here on out things are going to be awkward as hell. We'll be back to hating one another.

"Here's the thing, Jaxon," I say as snarkily as I can. "I am just not all that into you." *Biggest lie ever!* "I haven't been with a man in a long time"—*truth there*—"and well, I lost control is all. A little like the other night. But believe me when I tell you that I really don't want *you*."

Oh, when his face falls, the pain that I feel. It's like his heart is in my chest. I hate myself right now.

Bristling, he jumps up from the sofa, his eyes flashing emerald fire as he turns to me.

Softly and—make no mistake about it—dangerously, he hisses, "Is that so, eh?"

I squeak out, "Uh-huh."

He takes a step toward me. "Then maybe you should think about leaving the island, Cara," he growls. "I'd hate to see you *lose control* a second time and not have any outlet. It could happen too, seeing as your sex drought *clearly* has no end in sight."

"Uh," I flounder. I don't even know how to respond to something like that.

Turns out, I don't have to.

Jaxon breaks into a wicked grin and snaps, "Do you want to know *why* you'll not have an outlet if you ever lose control again?"

"Um, I'm not sure where you're going with this, but okay, I'll bite.

Why?"

"Because, Cara..." He closes the gap between us with one long stride, making my breath catch in my throat. "Let me assure you that after today I will never, ever lay a finger on you." He leans forward and breathes in my ear, sending delicious shivers down my spine. "Not even if you're the last woman on this planet."

"Jaxon," I try to protest.

But he's having none of it as he says, "Just remember, you chose this. And you will never have my cock."

My chest heaves, my nipples grow taut. My body is practically begging for his touch. This closeness, his words, I want him now more than ever.

Too bad I just fucked up my one and only shot.

17

THIS IS WAR

JAXON

This is war. I'm done being nice. She doesn't fucking want me? Bullshit. Her body tells a different story, even now.

Like I can't see her nipples hardening or feel her quickened breaths.

"It's too late, sweetheart," I say, smirking before I turn and walk away.

"W-where are you going?" she calls out from behind me.

"Wherever you aren't," I lob back, like a grenade, over my shoulder.

I swear I even hear my words exploding behind me.

Wait, that's something shattering for real.

Shit, Cara just threw something at me, and thankfully missed.

I spin around to find the decorative bud vase that was on the coffee table less than a minute ago lying in pieces on the hardwood floor.

"Noel will expect you to pay for that," I snap. "He'll probably want money for the planter you destroyed too. You sure are a destructive houseguest, aren't you, Cara? Bet you *never* get invited back."

"Oh, shut up, Jaxon."

As she drops to her knees to clean up the broken glass, I can't help but remark, "That's a good look for you, by the way. You on your hands and knees like a good little girl. I like it."

Harsh words, yes, but this is war, remember?

Hey, at least I only throw verbal shots, not actual projectiles that could do real damage.

I expect to have some other breakable item tossed my way, but instead Cara spits out, "Go to Hell."

"Already there, devil woman."

Ooh, if looks could kill.

"Asshole," she murmurs.

"So," I taunt, "are you finally ready to call the airline and book that flight out of here?"

"*I'm* not leaving." Ooh, she's digging in. "Why don't you go? After all, who'd want to be stuck in Hell with a devil woman, right?"

I laugh at her sugar-sweet yet venomous tone. I'll give her credit, she can spar. But I can too, with the best of them.

"Don't worry, honey, I like it hot. Remember when you asked me that? Well, hell is fine with me. Hate to break it to you, but *I'm* not going anywhere."

Does she really think I'd capitulate so easily? No way. There'll be no white flags going up in this camp, not on my watch.

And sure, I suspect there'll be some battles lost here and there, but make no mistake about it—I will fucking win this war.

The next morning, I make an interesting discovery. Mr. Hockeypants has removed the post bashing me. Plus all the comments on the new post have been removed. Even better, the commenting function on the whole shitty blog has been disabled.

That puts me in a better mood.

Still, erring on the side of caution, I decide to contact my attorney.

I won't go after the site for removal, but I'd like to know who is behind the mask of anonymity.

I just need to know who Mr. Hockeypants really is so I can confront the prick when I get back to Vegas.

18

SUNBURNED AND BURNED

CARA

The next few days pass with me and Jaxon pretty much avoiding each other. It's worse than that short period of time when we weren't speaking. Now we eat at completely different times and sit yards apart when we're down on the beach.

I even start turning my big yellow and black striped umbrella so it hides him more than it shields me from the sun. I get a certain satisfaction in viewing it like it's a big imaginary bee aimed at him, poised to sting.

Too bad I'm the one who ends up getting stung.

Not by a bee, but by the sun.

Despite applying copious amounts of sunscreen, and having a solid base tan, I end up sunburned all to hell.

Back inside the house later that day, I'm dancing around my

bedroom in pain, hissing, "Ouch, ouch, ouch."

Yep, I just peeled away my bikini top to reveal two brightly burned shoulders and a mean red streak running down between my boobs, spots I neglected to apply enough sunscreen to.

Damn Jaxon.

If I hadn't had to point my umbrella in his direction, I would've been fine. But I really had no choice in the matter. He was looking way too hot today, and not because it was close to ninety degrees.

His body is already a beautiful bronze shade, even though he sits under an umbrella himself most days. But today I swear he looked like a damn god sitting there, sculpted and wet after emerging from an impromptu dip in the ocean.

Fuuuuuck…

I need a cold shower just thinking about him. Since it'll help my sunburn, I go ahead and take one, keeping the water turned to ice cold. That helps both of my problems, sunburn and horniness.

After drying off, I throw on a pair of skimpy navy boy shorts and a sky blue tube top. Then I cautiously head downstairs for a much-needed snack.

I stop at the base, listening for signs of Jaxon.

Hmm, there's no noise coming from the kitchen. I think I'm safe.

"Thank God," I murmur. "I can eat in peace."

Then again, maybe not. Just as I'm rounding the corner, I run headlong into my enemy.

"Damn it, Holland." I jump back like I've been burned with a hot poker. "Could you make your presence known? You're like a freaking ninja some days."

Looking surprised, and dare I say kind of pleased, he says, "Shit, Milne, that may be the nicest thing you've said to me in days."

"It's the *only* thing I've said to you in days," I remind him.

He looks at me then.

And I look at him.

Oooh, there's still a war waging for sure.

But then it's like we both suddenly realize what we have on.

Or more like what we *don't* have on.

Thin sweat shorts for him and nothing else—*gah!*—and that tube top and boy shorts for me.

I stand quietly and just blatantly gawk at the man.

Doesn't matter, he's doing the same to me.

This is the closest we've been in days, and it's like I can smell every delicious thing about him, enemy or not.

I give in a little bit and inhale.

Mmm, Jaxon is spicy and male and full of the promise of delicious sex—

"Jesus, what the hell happened to your shoulders?" he blurts out, ruining my budding fantasy.

The look of lust that was percolating in his gaze turns to concern.

Noooo, don't be nice.

My resolve is strengthened only through our unrequited sexual tension and anger at each other. Let that fall away and I might cave.

But no, no, *no*, I can't lose when it comes to him. Losing would mean more than simply him winning. It would mean I'd be free—to want him, to touch him, to kiss him.

And it wouldn't stop there.

But we all know why that can't happen.

Despite our battling, he doesn't really hate me. But he would if he knew the truth. He'd find out too, as I'd *have* to tell him if we grew any closer. I just couldn't keep my blog identity a secret if we were intimate.

So yeah, hating each other like this is better.

Huffing indignantly, I cross my arms—*ow!*—and snap back, "I clearly have a sunburn, genius. And for the record, it's *your* fault."

"Oh"—he crosses his arms too—"this should be good. Do explain how it's *my* fault."

"Well, if you hadn't insisted on lying out on the beach at the same time I chose to be there—"

"What? You mean when the freaking sun is out? Because if so, that's when most people lay out, *genius*."

Ooh, throwing my words back at me. Clever, but not effective.

I wave him off. "Irrelevant. You could always lie out on the patio."

He chuffs, "You'd still have to pass me on your way down to the beach."

"I'd just run. And maybe even close my eyes."

"Pfft, and take the chance that I'd trip you."

"Oh, you...you..."

I place my hands on my hips. That's much better than having them crossed over my sore chest. Scrunching up sunburned skin is not a good idea.

Now where was I?

Ah, yes, he threatened to trip me.

I narrow my eyes at him. "You wouldn't dare, Jaxon Holland."

He smirks. "Would you really want to take a chance and find out, sweetheart?"

"Grrr, I hate you so much right now!" I stomp my foot and *shiiiit*—my tube top slips down!

Now I'm totally flashing him, not that he seems to mind.

"Help," I squeak out.

Jaxon doesn't help. He's too busy staring hungrily at my boobs.

Huffing, I yank up my tube top and...*fuuuck!*

"That hurts like Satan's fury!" I bellow.

Now that my boobs are covered and no longer a distraction, Jaxon magically regains his voice.

"Makes sense," he sneers, "seeing as you are a devil woman."

"Jaxon," I sigh. "Just shut up already."

I drop my hand from where I've just abraded the tender skin between my boobs. And when I wince, he finally seems to get it that I'm really hurting here.

Softening, he says, "You should put some ice on that sunburn, plus maybe rub in a little aloe vera gel."

Typical of him, trying to be all helpful after the damage is already done.

"I don't need your input," I snap.

Immediately, I feel bad. He's only trying to help now. And I could kind of use a friend. I mean, how else am I going to get aloe vera on the backs of my shoulders?

"Can we call a truce?" I whisper.

He raises a brow. "Sure you want to do that, soldier?"

"It'd only be temporary, just for tonight."

"Okay."

I'm relieved, but why does it feel like I just lost a battle?

19

SIDE BOOB ACTION AND A THONG

JAXON

I can do a truce. Only for tonight, though, just like we agreed.

I wouldn't want it to last any longer, anyway. Cara hasn't earned any more reprieve than that.

Maybe I still feel slighted that she rejected me. I guess I do since, bristling at the memory, I squeeze the tube of aloe vera gel I'm holding a little too hard and a big glop of goo lands smack-dab between Cara's shoulder blades.

Shuddering, she murmurs, "Ooh, that's cold, Jaxon."

"Sorry," I say.

Not really, I think.

"Mmm, it feels good, though, where I'm sunburned."

Eh, so much for that victory.

And then it kind of hits me, the scene before me.

Damn, I deserve a pat on the back for my incredible restraint. Not only is Cara lying facedown on the sofa with her tube top pulled down to her waist, she's sporting some serious side boob action. Plus, her ass cheeks are hanging out of those skimpy boy shorts, tempting me, taunting me.

God, give me strength.

I need to think of something snide to say. It's easier to hate her when we're fighting.

Luckily, I do think of something, and it's such a good one that I have to laugh.

"What's so funny, Jaxon?" Cara murmurs into the back of the sofa. Her head is turned that way.

Here we go…

"I was just thinking how you really do look like a devil woman right now, what with all the red skin. You just need some horns and a tail and you're good to go."

It backfires on me right away. She doesn't even seem that mad. And now I can't stop staring at her ass and those perfectly rounded cheeks without thinking of a tail.

Damn, she'd look hot in one of those sexy devil costumes at Halloween.

Focus, Jaxon!

"Ha-ha," she snorts. "You think you're so funny, don't you?"

Gruffly, I snap, "Like you thought you were funny when you turned your umbrella toward me? Look at where that got you."

Ooh, that pisses her off.

"That's it. I'm out of here." She sits up, turning away so she can pull up her tube top without me catching a shot of her tits.

I do catch something, though—her wincing in pain. And that makes me feel like shit.

"Hey, hey, don't leave. I shouldn't have said that," I say.

She turns around, her hurt eyes meeting my apologetic ones.

"Then why did you?" she asks.

I shrug. "I don't know. I guess I forgot that we called a truce."

"Clearly."

"Hey, just lie back down. I promise to be nice."

Huffing, she resumes her position, shimmying down her tube top to her waist once more.

Great, the side-boob action now includes some bouncing. *Fuck me.* I'm glad she doesn't turn her head and catch me adjusting my junk.

"Okay, I'm ready," she murmurs into the cushions.

Yeah, so am I, I think, adjusting myself once more.

Sighing, I pour a big glob of gel onto my palm, then start rubbing it gently onto her sunburned shoulders.

After a minute of that, she says, "Wow, you really do have a way with your hands, Jaxon. Guess that's why you're such a good hockey player, huh?"

Wow, a rare compliment.

"Guess so," I mumble.

That's nice, but she really needs to experience the "way" I have with my hands when I'm doing *other* things. She thinks this feels good? Ha.

Well, it's her loss. She chose this path.

Clearing my throat, I say, "I told you I could be nice."

She turns and peers up at me with hard-to-read hazel eyes. "I like when you're nice. It's been tough with us lately, hasn't it?"

"It has," I concur.

Crap, I have to break the eye contact, as the spell it weaves, even while we're at war, is too intense and disconcerting.

"Hey, this truce is only temporary," I remind her.

"Yes." She hides her face back in the cushions. "It's only for tonight, I know. We can get back to hating each other tomorrow."

Is that regret I hear in her tone?

I don't know, but now is not the time to get into it, in any way, shape, or form. She has sunburn and I'm simply trying to help.

The fact that I can't keep my eyes off her boobs and ass as I continue to apply aloe vera to her skin is irrelevant.

Yeah, dude, keep telling yourself that.

After Cara goes up to bed, I stay downstairs, lounging on the sofa. It's still warm from her body, which I like.

Needing a distraction, I take out my phone and check for messages.

There's nothing in the form of voice mails or texts, but there is an email from my attorney. He's closing in on Mr. Hockeypants. Seems the dude is hiding behind a phony IP registered in a state up north.

Hmm, it may take a little while longer, but I know nothing will stop my guy. He's ruthless.

Just like I plan to be once I find out the true identity of Mr. Hockeypants.

20

A WORTHY ADVERSARY

CARA

My sunburn feels much better the next day. Still, I know I should stay indoors.

Hunkering down in my bed with my trusty tablet, I get set to spend the day catching up on novels.

I'm wearing the same boy shorts and tube top I had on last night. I fell asleep in them and see no sense in changing. I'll just shower later.

With that decided, I start reading. But not twenty minutes into it, just as I'm getting into a super-steamy love scene, there's a knock on my door.

"What?" I yell.

It's Jaxon, of course. "Just checking to see if you're okay in there," he says loudly. "Do you need anything?"

That sex scene must be affecting me because I almost yell back, *just you and that big glorious cock of yours.*

"Cara?"

Jesus, must his voice sound so sexy and suggestive when he says my name? That just encourages these X-rated thoughts.

Or is it the novel making me think these things?

Damn hot book sex.

I should've chosen a Stephen King selection. Even creepy clowns are preferable to feeling like I'm about to attack my hot-ass housemate, who I'm back at war with.

Jaxon raps on the door again, and I scream, "I'm fine, I'm fine. I don't need a thing!"

Except for that hot throbbing piece of man meat I saw the first day I met you.

"Are you sure?" Jaxon yells back. "You sound kind of…funny."

Great. Nice to know my I-want-hot-sex-from-you-now-Jaxon voice sounds "funny" to him.

I swear some days you're the windshield, and other days you're the bug. This is definitely shaping up to be a bug kind of day for me.

Why else would I feel like I was just swatted down by Jaxon Holland?

He really needs to go.

But he sounds like he's sticking around out there, probably waiting for me to open the door.

Well, drastic times call for drastic measures.

"I have cramps," I yell extra loud. "My period just started."

Total silence, as I expected.

No wait, there's a scuffling noise, probably him backing slowly away from the door.

Ha, period talk works like a charm every time. No man wants to engage in menstrual musings. They just don't know what to say.

But Jaxon's no ordinary man. He breaks all the freaking rules. As proven when he yells back, "Aw, I'm sorry to hear that. That sucks. I have some muscle relaxants in my room, though. Would you like one?"

Ugh, this man, thwarting my attempt to throw him off. I'm not even on my period. That came and went days ago. I can pretty much set my clock by my cycle these days. Exactly what I was hoping for when I went on the pill a few months ago. Dealing with irregular cycles really blows!

But back to Jaxon—I kind of do want to see how good he looks today. It'll be prime fodder to fuel the fantasy I'm planning on re-igniting once I'm alone again.

So, sighing, I call out, "Sure, I'll take one of those muscle relaxants."

I don't add in that I'll just hold on to it for the next time I really do have cramps.

He yells then that he'll be right back.

"Cool," I say.

I then immediately jump up so I can fluff out my hair and make sure my boobs are boosted to maximum cleavage in the tube top. I may as well give Jaxon a little fuel for his own fantasies, right? I don't want to be the only one living in lust around here.

Though I suspect I'm not.

Ah, the dangerous game we're playing.

The truce was a bad idea, I know that now. Jaxon touching me last night while I was half-dressed was too much. Coupled with hot book sex this morning, I'm wavering.

I'm even thinking of giving in.

But I can't.

I'm Mr. freaking Hockeypants.

Jaxon returns and I open the door.

Dammmn.

He looks better than I expected. His body's all pumped up, like he was working out this morning.

Staring at his ripped abs and firm chest, I blurt out, "Did you find a weight room in the house or something?"

His eyes trail up from where he was doing a little staring of his own.

"Interesting that you should notice," he purrs. Yes, purrs, people. *Purrs!* "Guess knocking out a few hundred push-ups on the floor in my room this morning paid off."

Show-off!

He's so smug.

He thinks he's winning this battle?

No way!

"Actually, I only asked because you look a little sweaty," I reply sugar-sweetly. Scrunching my nose, I add, "Ew, you smell a little off too."

He's not sweaty, and he definitely doesn't smell "off." He smells *delicious.* I could just eat him up, if only things were different.

He looks genuinely worried, though, like what I just said might be true.

But after he sees my *got-you* smirk, he knows this war is just ramping up.

Proving himself a worthy adversary, he snarks, "Hmm, I always heard the sense of smell is heightened when women have their, uh, time." He falters for a second there but quickly composes himself. "Guess it must be true. But don't fret, Cara." He presses the pill into my hand, his fingers lingering. "I'll head back down the hall now so I can take a long, hot, steaming"—I yank my hand away—"shower."

"Mmm-hmm," I cough. "Yeah, you do that."

"Sure you don't want to join me?"

Holy hell, I almost say yes. Seems for as much as I hate Jaxon Holland, I really like him.

That's why I do the only thing I can in order to maintain my last shred of dignity—I slam the door in his face.

21

I DON'T SMELL!

JAXON

I don't smell. I took a shower!

Even though I know Cara was just yanking my chain, I feel compelled to check my pits as I'm walking away from the door she just slammed in my face.

One thing for sure—looks like our temporary truce is officially over.

Fuck, she drives me nuts.

She's so difficult, and not a good liar at all. I mean, come on, does she really think for a minute I bought her my-period-started story?

Riiight.

Like I didn't see a tampon wrapper in the downstairs powder room just last week? I only went along with her today to fuck with her. And, of course, to let her know I'm not so easily rattled.

Bottom line, Cara needs to work on her tactics. It's going to take a little more than some not-even-real blood to win a round with me.

Speaking of which, I think I won this one. Her slamming the door in my face is akin to retreat from the battlefield. She may as well have tucked her tail and ran.

I know for sure I won when she remains in her room the whole day.

She doesn't emerge the following day either.

I get the feeling she thinks she's punishing me, but I'm not as alone as she's probably hoping.

First, the housekeeper comes by on the first day of Cara's exile to do a little cleaning and to drop off a fresh supply of groceries.

I make small talk with the nice, matronly lady. She tells me about her toddler-age great-grandkids and how she loves them, but they drive her crazy some days. I tell her about an adult-age woman who makes me pretty crazy too.

"You have feelings for this woman?" she asks with an all-too-knowing smile.

Do I? "Good God, no!"

"You're just friends, then?"

I think about Cara locked away in her bedroom, avoiding me, and mutter dejectedly, "Not even that."

Housekeeper lady just shakes her head.

The groundskeeper stops in the next day. He's a crotchety old fellow of about eighty.

Good. He won't inquire about my "feelings" for Cara or anything uncomfortable like that. That means it's safe to talk with him.

I follow him around, chatting away, as he completes various tasks around the house.

Guess not having Cara around to talk to is taking a toll after all.

The groundskeeper isn't much company, though. He's all business, making sure everything is in tip-top order. He's also totally fixated on the little lizards out back, especially around the patio area.

I assure him that the lizards don't bother me or Cara, like at all.

But he insists, "Those creatures can become quite the nuisance, sir."

"Yeah, maybe, but my housemate really likes them," I counter.

"That may be. But, sir, I must do my job."

He turns away and gets to work on setting out what look to be small glue traps.

Appalled, I protest again. But he insists the lizards can be released humanely from the traps with a little oil.

Still, this doesn't seem right. Like Cara, I really like those little guys. Not to mention, this is absolutely not going to fly with her. If any ends up hurt—or God forbid worse—Cara will freak the hell out.

So as soon as I see the groundskeeper leave, I walk around the back patio and flower gardens, collecting all the traps so I can throw them away.

Afterward, since I'm back to being bored as hell, I decide to take a run on the beach.

I need to anyway. It's never too early to start training for the upcoming season. Time passes quickly, and next thing you know, training camp will be here.

Okay, it's not till September, but still. I plan to head back to Vegas in early August. I'm already starting to miss working out on the ice. So that means I only have about a month left at this island paradise.

Jeez, I sure hope Cara and I are on better terms before I leave. I don't know why it's important to me that we are, but it is. I guess because I'd really like to stay in touch with her once we're both back in Nevada.

She may drive me crazy, but I really do like her.

To be honest, I like her *a lot.*

I guess the housekeeper was right—I do have feelings for Cara. And even though we're not on good terms, they seem to be growing.

Fuck.

NEVER WILL I EVER...

CARA

The self-imposed exile in my bedroom lasts all of two days.

Jaxon doesn't know it, but I already snuck downstairs once or twice when he was out on the beach. I was just too darn hungry to make it straight through.

Little surprise then that, when hunger strikes again on the morning of day three, I am once again sneaking down to the kitchen, though not nearly as carefully as my former forays.

I don't know why. I guess it's just so quiet I assume my enemy must be out back.

But when I skulk into the kitchen, surprise!

There's Jaxon.

Gulp.

He looks smoking hot, as usual, in long shorts and a black tee that clings to his sculpted muscles the way I'd like to.

Wait, no.

When he notices me just standing in the doorway, he snidely exclaims, "Wow, she lives. It's a miracle."

Since I know he just totally caught me staring at his pecs, I force my eyes up to his face, my cheeks flaming.

"Uh, I didn't realize you were down here," I mutter, spinning around to leave. "It's okay, though. I can come back later."

I'm all set to make this grand exit, but then my stomach growls, protesting so loudly that Jaxon surely hears.

He chuckles. And I brace myself for a nasty remark.

But instead, softly and not unkindly, he says, "Hey, there's no need to run off, Cara. Stay."

My stomach begs me to give in, so I turn around and acquiesce. "Okay."

I step into the kitchen but falter when Jaxon quips, "You must be feeling better. I was beginning to think you might never come out of that room."

"Hmm, I bet you'd like that," I can't help but mutter under my breath.

Squaring up his shoulders, he says, "What was that now?"

I square up my own T-shirt-clad shoulders, though my shirt is bubblegum pink, not exactly a color that demands respect.

"It was nothing important," I say. "And for your information, I am feeling much better."

"Well, that's good."

Jaxon hits a button on the blender sitting on the counter. He's whipping up what looks to be, and smells like, a peanut butter smoothie.

I love peanut butter anything, so no surprise that my mouth begins to water.

"That looks really good," I say, hoping he'll share.

Turning off the blender, he says, "It is, Cara. And you want to know something I once heard? It's really fascinating and may even apply to you."

Uh-oh. I have a feeling I'm about to walk into a minefield. But I don't care. I want some of that freaking smoothie.

So I bite.

"What did you hear?"

"I heard that peanut butter is *really* good for cramps."

I narrow my eyes at him. He knows the truth. He knows I wasn't on my period.

Quietly, I murmur, "I don't have cramps."

"You don't?" He feigns surprise. *Smartass.* "Hmm, well, okay."

I can't believe we're discussing this. Where's my invitation to share the smoothie with him?

Since it's clearly not forthcoming, I just go ahead and ask, "Can I have some?"

"What? You want some of this smoothie, even though you don't have cramps?"

Quit playing dumb.

"Yes, Jaxon, I do."

"Sure. You can have as much as you want. But first…" He reaches under the counter. "I have one more key ingredient to add."

"Key ingredient?" I murmur.

"Yep."

To my horror, he holds up an egg, smirking evilly.

Oh, no you don't!

My eyes burn into his, urging him not to do it.

But he just keeps on smiling.

Cracking the egg in his hand like a pro chef, he proceeds to dump raw yolk and egg white into the blender.

"Noooo!" I cry out.

He plays innocent. "What? It needs more protein."

He hits another button and the blender whirs to life, effectively shutting me up.

But I'm not so easily silenced.

Rolling my eyes, I stomp over to the refrigerator.

"That's just great!" I scream over the noise. "You totally ruined it. I don't want any now."

He laughs victoriously. "Fine. It's your loss. That just means there's more for me."

I swear I'm going to get him back for this. Maybe I'll add hot sauce to the next smoothie he makes. Though knowing him, he'll probably like it.

"It'll give it more protein," I mock.

The blender stops. "Were you saying something, Cara?"

"To you?" I spin around, hands on my hips. "Absolutely not." I pause for a sec, then add, "No, wait, I do have something to say—"

But he hits the blender button again, drowning me out.

Jerk.

"Ugh, I hate you!" I yell.

And then I storm out.

I can't get back to my room fast enough.

I slam the door behind me, even though Jaxon is downstairs and can't hear a thing. And then, stomping my foot, I scream, "That man frustrates the fuck out of me!"

And just why is that, Cara? a little voice asks inside my head.

"Oh, shut up," I grumble.

My phone buzzes then.

Thank God, saved by the bell.

It's Noelle, so I answer right away.

We talk and soon I'm feeling better. Even boring details about her internship are preferable to thinking about jerky Jaxon.

But then she brings him up.

"So how are things going with you and your roomie?"

"He's not my roomie," I snap. "We don't share a bedroom, God forbid."

Noelle says, "Well, all righty then."

Sighing, I apologize for being so snippy. "I don't know what's wrong with me."

"That's okay, Cara," she says.

I then admit, "Truthfully, things are a mess with Jaxon. I think we may end up killing each other."

Noelle reads the situation like a pro.

"Ooh, sounds to me like there's lots of pent-up sexual tension brewing. That could be fun. You two should do it and just get it out of your systems."

"That is *never* going to happen," I grind out.

"Ha, we'll see," she retorts.

Adamantly, I state, "Seriously, Noelle, I would never sleep with Jaxon freaking Holland."

She laughs. "Who said anything about sleeping?"

"Just stop."

She doesn't, of course.

"I don't know, Cara. If you ask me, it sounds like there may be more than sexual tension brewing between you two."

Horrified, I snap back, "What's that supposed to mean?"

"It means maybe you're developing real feelings for each other."

"Oh, God forbid." I bark out a laugh and assure her, "Never will I ever develop real feelings for that insufferable man."

"Yeah, you just keep telling yourself that."

I want to be mad and dispute her, but the problem is that she's right.

23

LIZARD RESCUE 911

JAXON

You'd think Cara having emerged from her exile would mean I'd see her all the time, like before.

But that doesn't happen.

What occurs instead is that she continues to avoid me like the plague. I guess adding egg to my peanut butter smoothie really ticked her off, just like I knew it would. That's why I did it.

But now I'm thinking maybe the joke's on me.

I miss Cara.

Though I'd never let her know. Nope, I just go about my business like I don't have a care in the world.

Too bad I do have a care, a big one—her.

That's not good, since I know for a fact she now hates me.

I don't require any more proof than when she comes down to

the beach the next day, sees me soaking up sun in a lounge chair, and promptly turns around and stomps back up to the patio.

"Hey, it's cooler down here by the water," I call out to her. "There's a really nice breeze today."

"Great," she throws back over her shoulder. "Maybe it'll blow you away."

"Ha, if any blowing occurs," I murmur to myself, chuckling, "I'd rather it be from you."

Shit, I do.

I *really* do, especially as I'm watching her cute, hot pink bikini-clad ass bopping up the wooden patio steps. I swear it's like she knows I'm gawking. Why else would she turn around and shoot me the bird.

This woman.

I shake my head and wave at her. But that just infuriates her further. *Good.*

She plops down on a chair that's partially hidden by the patio wall and a bunch of those ubiquitous freaking planters, so I can't see much of her now.

"Damn." I turn back to face the turquoise water, and that's when I realize I'm sporting some pretty impressive wood.

Cara is going to be the death of me if I don't eventually get to have her. Or maybe I just need to get laid in general. Too bad Cara's the only female on the island. Well, besides the housekeeper. But she's about seventy, so yeah, no. That'd exceed even my top-range cougar limit.

So we're back to Cara.

Too bad she's not an option. With our off-the-charts sexual chemistry, kindled by our never-ending fighting, I just know sex with her would be amazing. We could fuck and fight, fuck and fight. She's like a hockey player's wet dream. Well, she's *this* hockey player's wet dream.

Consumed with thoughts of Cara, which I really need to put a stop to, I close my eyes and drift off to fantasyland.

But suddenly, out of the blue, I'm awoken by a bloodcurdling scream from up on the patio.

What the fuck?

Next there's a loud barrage of "Help, help!" cries.

God, no! That's Cara!

I fly out of the chair and race up to the patio. But it's like a nightmare getting there. The sand is thick and deep, slowing me down.

"Jaxon, please, hurry."

"I'm coming, Cara. Hold on."

I finally get through the sand and clamber up the wooden steps to find Cara standing in the middle of the patio, her bronzed body shaking.

"What's wrong?" I ask, since I see nothing amiss.

She points to a corner of the patio. "Look over there."

I peer down. There are two side-by-side planters, but nothing looks out of the ordinary.

Oh, no, maybe poor Cara has sunstroke.

"Uh, those are just planters," I say slowly, like I'm talking to a toddler.

"I know that," she snaps, waving her hand impatiently. "Look between them, you fool."

"Fool?"

She blows out a breath. "Okay, I didn't mean that. But look again, Jaxon, to the right of the big terra-cotta pot. Do you see it now?"

I look, see nothing off, and murmur a questioning, "Um, no?"

Cara grows impatient. "Jaxon, look closer. How can you not see that a poor little lizard is stuck in some kind of a-a...*trap*."

She spits out the last word like it's poison on her tongue.

And finally I see what she's referring to—there's a small green lizard stuck, struggling in the gloppy glue of one of those infernal traps.

"Damn it all to hell," I grind out as I crouch down to get a better look. "I knew this would happen. That's why I got rid of those things. Or so I thought..."

"Where'd a trap like that even come from?" Cara asks as she moves to stand behind me.

"The groundskeeper put a bunch of them out the day he was here."

"But why?" she queries.

"Apparently, he thinks the lizards are pests."

Cara's spitting mad now.

"That's bullshit, Jaxon. And even if they were, they're God's little creatures and have a right to be here too. In fact, they were probably on this island before anyone ever built anything."

Wow, she sure is passionate. I wish I could tell her to release that passion on me. But that'd probably end with another one of her self-imposed exiles. And I don't want that.

So I just agree, "I'm sure they were."

Cara's not done yet, though.

"Didn't you inform the groundskeeper that we don't believe in inhumane things like glue traps?"

We've actually never discussed it, but I find it endearing that she knows we're on the same page—which, of course, we are.

"I did," I reply. "But he put them out anyway."

Like she's just remembering what I said earlier, she murmurs in awe, "And you went around and threw them all away?"

Whoa, what's that I hear? Is it appreciation for my forward

thinking? I think it might be.

And then I know for sure that it is when I glance up and Cara's smiling down at me. It's a nice genuine smile too, not a smirk or a wicked grin.

"I did," I confirm. "But I must have missed one."

"Still, that was very sweet of you, Jaxon," she quietly states.

Not being a smartass at all, I reply with a sincere, "Thanks."

Nodding to the lizard, who is peering up at us with frightened, beady eyes, she says, "Do you think you can save him?"

"I think so, sweetheart."

Wow, that's like the first time I've used that term of endearment in a non-snarky way.

I have to laugh. Leave it to a lizard to bring us together. Perhaps I should *thank* the groundskeeper.

Filing that away as something to consider for later, I get to work on the task at hand—saving the trapped lizard.

"We're going to need some oil," I tell her.

"What kind?" Cara asks.

I glance around and spot the bottle of baby oil that's over on the ground by her chair.

Gesturing, I say, "That one should do."

I guess our reprieve from arguing is over, since we get into a heated debate over what kind of oil to use. She thinks the baby oil is no good.

"His skin might burn once he's back in the sun, Jaxon."

"He's a leathery reptile," I counter. "He spends his whole day in the sun."

"Yes," she agrees, "but he doesn't do so with baby oil slathered all over his little body."

I roll my eyes. "I wasn't planning on *slathering* him in it, Cara. I was just going to use a drop or two to help free him."

She huffs. "I just don't know. I thought it'd be okay for me to use baby oil today, seeing as I have such a good base tan, but look at me now. I'm already a little pink."

She leans over to where I'm crouched.

Great.

Here I am trying to be her gentlemanly knight in shining armor, and she's directing my attention to her shapely breasts, which are totally spilling out of her skimpy bikini top...and in my freaking face!

Fuck gentlemanly.

Perv that I so clearly am, I say, "Can you lean in a little closer? I can't really tell."

Not catching on to my wicked ways, she complies and her absolutely luscious tits are so close now that if I were to lean forward, even an inch, I could wrap my mouth around the nipple that's peeking over the edge of her bikini top on the left side.

But no, wait.

I shake my head.

Now is not the time for making moves. We have a situation here, and a golden opportunity for me to be a hero. If I play my cards right, I could have those delectable mounds in my mouth every single night, along with some other surely equally delectable parts of Cara.

She'll want to reward her knight in shining armor, right?

So I restrain my urges and just stare at her skin. "Yeah, it's a little reddish."

"See!" She straightens victoriously, adjusting her top. *Damn.* "Baby oil won't work for the lizard," she declares.

"Okay, okay. What do you suggest instead?"

"I don't know. Let me get my phone. We can google it."

We do exactly that and discover we're going to need more than oil for this operation. To free the lizard in a safe manner for all involved, we'll need vegetable oil, dish soap, and a deep plastic bowl.

After Cara finds those items in the house, I spread them out in front of us. But before I can dive in to the rescue operation, she stops me.

"Wait, there's one more thing." She hands me a thick pair of gardening gloves and smiles kindly. Not wickedly or like she's up to something, just a cute caring smile.

"You don't want to get bit, Jaxon."

"No, that wouldn't be good."

I slip on the gloves, appreciative of her thoughtfulness. "Where'd you find these, anyway?" I ask.

She points to around the side of the house. "The groundskeeper keeps a supply box over there. I noticed it a long time ago. Anyway, I figured there'd be gloves in there."

"That was some smart thinking," I say. "Thanks."

"You're welcome, Jaxon."

We share a smile, and then I take a deep breath and get started on freeing the lizard.

It goes really well. The oil, of which I use only a dab, helps to free his little feet. Of course, he then attempts to run away.

"Wait, you're not done yet, little buddy."

I grab hold of him and place him in the plastic bowl so we can clean him off. It's like a coordinated operation now. We're a real rescue team.

Cara hands me the dish soap so I can clean off the excess oil from our little friend. I keep the gloves on, even though he doesn't try to bite me. I think he knows we're trying to help him.

But still, better safe than sorry.

After we rinse off his feet with a trickle of water from the hose, we let him go, proclaiming the operation a success.

That night, I call Noel. He's none too happy to learn of the groundskeeper's actions.

"Don't worry," he tells me. "I'll make sure he knows not to ever again put out any kind of lizard trap."

I'm glad, but what's more important is Cara will be pleased. I like seeing her happy, and I like doing things for her. She may drive me crazy, but it's time to admit that she really does mean something to me.

I just need to figure out exactly what.

24

WHO NEEDS FOOD WHEN YOU HAVE LOVE?

CARA

I can't deny that Jaxon saving the lizard melts my heart.

He's not a bad guy after all. He's a sweet and caring man.

I think I've always known that in my heart. But if that's true, why do we fight so much?

"I don't know," I murmur to myself as I'm blow-drying my sun-highlighted hair.

I'm up in the bathroom that's connected to my bedroom, readying to head back downstairs.

After the successful lizard-saving operation, Jaxon suggested we indulge in a celebratory dinner. I agreed but wanted to shower and change first. He said he would like to do the same.

But he's clearly beaten me, seeing as the savory aromas of burgers on the grill are wafting up to my bedroom.

I sigh.

That man sure can cook, which is another plus in his favor.

"Wait." I stop and stare at my reflection in the mirror. "Why am I counting up all the good things about Jaxon Holland?"

Better not answer that.

No. I stop myself. Not this time. I am going to answer the question, damn it. It's high time I admit I have feelings for Jaxon, like *real* feelings. I just don't know if I should act upon them. For obvious reasons—can you say Mr. Hockeypants?

As I shimmy into a bright yellow, crisscross-backed sundress, I accept that the only thing holding me back is the same as before—my secret blog identity.

If I just tell him, it'd no longer be a concern.

But what if it doesn't go well?

Then we're back to square one.

See, this is where I always stall. I'm scared to death of his reaction. And I'm afraid of the fallout.

"We're getting nowhere here," I grumble as I leave my room and start down the stairs.

Little wonder that by the time I'm walking into the kitchen, I'm chewing my lip, consumed by worry and confusion on how to proceed.

Since not much goes unnoticed by Jaxon, he glances up from where he's plating burgers, catches me nibbling at my lip, and says, "Is everything okay, Cara?"

"Yes, yes." I wave my hand like I'm sweeping away his concern. "I'm just overthinking crap is all."

He raises a brow. "Care to elaborate?"

Is he nuts? "I don't think so."

"All right, but you know overthinking shit isn't always bad. Not if you can reach a resolution on whatever it is that's bothering you."

I realize that's the problem—I never reach a resolution. I just overthink, overanalyze, and end up back at square one.

Fuck it.

I'm going with my gut from now on.

"You know what," I proclaim, smiling like a loon. "You're absolutely right."

"Wow, you look rather happy all of a sudden," he says.

"I am, Jaxon," I confirm. "I am."

"Does this mean you reached a resolution?"

"I sure did. I decided to stop with all the overthinking and just go with what my heart's been telling me to do for a long time now."

Ooh, he looks really curious.

"What does that mean?" he asks, our eyes meeting.

I take a deep breath, and then I blurt out in a rush of words, "It means I'm tired of fighting the inevitable."

His eyes bore into me, and I swear he already knows what I mean. It's like he knows I'm referring to him…to *us*.

Swallowing hard, he steps out from behind the counter, looking gorgeous, as always. His hair's a little damp, making it appear darker than its usual sandy brown shade. He's wearing khaki shorts and a royal blue tee, which shows off his bronze skin perfectly. Jaxon's tan, like me, but so very buff, so freaking hard.

I watch as his defined leg muscles flex when he takes a purposeful step toward me.

When he's less than a foot away, he stops and rasps, "So what is your heart telling you to do at this very moment, Cara?"

I stare at his bare feet, tan like the rest of him. Then I glance up, chuckling nervously. "Uh, it's telling me to do a lot of things."

He whispers, "Name just one."

Just as softly, I respond, "Well, right now, my heart's telling me those burgers can wait."

He cocks a brow. "And...?"

"Hey, you said I only had to name one."

He shrugs. "I lied. Tell me one more."

It's time to be more honest with him than I've even been with myself.

I take a deep breath, and say, "My heart's telling me I should kiss the heck out of you right now, since you're so freaking close."

"Shit, sweetheart." He smiles. "I agree. Your heart is abso-fucking-lutely right."

I let go, in more ways than one. I take a freaking step forward and kind of fall into Jaxon. I trust him now, and I trust me. I'm also trusting that fate will let this all work out in the end.

But damn, even if it doesn't, this is still good. I'm about to have a fabulous experience, I'm sure.

And fabulous it is when Jaxon lowers his mouth to mine.

Yes.

Our lips meet hungrily, and his hand snakes into my hair, where he tightens and tugs in synchronization with the dance our tongues decide on.

At one point, I gasp into his mouth, "Unh, Jaxon," and he swallows my words like he's devouring the essence of me.

Pretty soon he's just straight-up devouring me, pulling up my dress, hoisting me onto the counter and urging me back.

I lie back and let him take the lead, which he does.

Swiftly, he slides my panties down my legs. He's like a man who knows what he's doing now...and knows what he wants. He's not going to let this get derailed.

It's intoxicating, this unbridled Jaxon. I guess he's letting his heart dictate his actions as well.

Good. I want wild abandon tonight on both our parts.

"More," I moan against his mouth when he resumes kissing me.

He stops long enough to rasp, "Oh, I have more for you, sweetheart. Don't you worry that pretty little head of yours."

He winks and disappears down my body.

"Wait, where are you going?" I say all innocently, like I don't know.

But then the games stop when I feel the heat of his tongue pressed to my clit.

"Oh, God…"

It's so good that I just about melt into the counter and fall apart right then and there. This has been such a long time coming. Jaxon Holland is actually down between my legs, doing sinfully delicious things with his mouth.

And then he adds a finger.

Gah!

"Does that feel good?" he asks, his lips vibrating against my swollen clit as he pauses.

"Yes, yes, yes, yes."

I think I get my point across since he chuckles, and then resumes what he was doing. And doing *so* well.

When I come apart, I scream out his name. I keep coming and coming, even when he stops. But when he sees me still shuddering, he shoves a finger back inside roughly, the way I need it now.

"Fuck, Jaxon…"

"That's right, baby. Keep coming for me."

I finally stop, but now I'm so open and ready for him. I'm like putty in his hands. And I want him to mold me.

"I want all of you, Jaxon," I cry out. "Please."

He nods and has me wrap my shaky legs and arms around him so he can carry me into the living room.

When he lets me down in front of the sofa, I stand on uneasy legs, like a newly born fawn.

Shakily, I raise my arms so he can lift my dress up and off of me. And then I regain some strength, enough to tug his shirt over his head while he's taking off his shorts.

When his cock springs free, rigid and hard, I just freaking stare and stare.

"Babe," he says, chuckling, "it's not like you haven't seen it before."

"Not up close like this," I remind him, a little breathless…and a lot impressed. "Plus, I'm kind of surprised you don't wear boxer briefs or some kind of underwear."

He laughs. "Back home I do, but I've been going commando around here."

"Mmm, maybe I should try that too," I muse.

"I highly encourage it, Cara." Jaxon drops to his knees. "It'll make it easier for me to do things like this at a moment's notice."

He closes his mouth over my pussy once more, his tongue working magic just like before.

I am definitely never wearing panties again!

He brings me to the brink, but doesn't let me go over the edge.

Standing, he says, "I want to be buried deep inside you when you come this next time."

"Oh, Jaxon, I want that too. But first I have one thing I want to do for you. It's my turn to…" I drop to my knees in front of him, wrapping my hand around his thick cock.

This is something I've wanted to do since the day I caught him outside touching himself.

"I want to play," I say, "like I saw you doing that first day."

I get no argument from him, not that I expected any.

So I play, experimenting, learning what he likes. I stroke and cup and try out different pressures. Jaxon likes them all, but he *loves* when I finally give up on hand stuff and take him in my mouth.

I'm sure to give him as much attention as he gave me, but I worry at one point that I might make him come. Jaxon, though, has amazing control and holds back.

But then he stops me and tells me it's time to move to the next level.

With me nodding, he lays me back on the sofa, and then settles his hard body between my legs.

But before we go any further, he says, "Hey, I want you to know that I'm clean. I'm always safe, Cara, and everyone on the team gets tested regularly. Still, I have condoms upstairs if you want me to go get some."

I love that he's telling me this. It makes my next decision easier.

With his heavy cock pressing into my folds—which feels incredible, by the way—I tell him, "No. I want to feel *all* of you, Jaxon. No barriers. I'm clean too. Plus I'm on the pill."

He blows out a breath. "So we're good?"

I nod. "We are."

I expect him to plunge into me, go all wild man on me, but he doesn't. He kisses my neck, my mouth, my breasts, while the length of him shifts, rubbing against my clit, teasing me, promising me that there's more to come.

I'm so wet and worked up by the time he reaches down to line us up that all he has to do is thrust his hips once and he's sheathed inside me.

"Ah, Jaxon…" I press my head back into the cushions. "You feel so fucking good."

"Not as good as you feel to me, sweetheart."

He starts to move then, a steady in and out, rhythmically fucking me. *Finally!* But it's more than just the culmination of all the weeks of fighting, getting along, and then fighting some more.

We thought we'd agreed to truces before, but this one is real.

Almost choking up, I move with him. I can tell Jaxon's trying not to get off too soon. He wants to prolong this, our first time, as much as I do.

"It's never been like this with anyone before," I whisper.

He lifts up so he can meet my eyes. "Good. I want to be your one and only, Cara. I want this to be special."

"Why is that, Jaxon?" I dare to ask.

He slows to a stop.

Buried deep inside me, he says, "I can think of only one reason. I've completely fallen for you."

"You have?"

"Yes." He laughs. "I am head-over-heels fucking crazy about you, okay?"

"Wow." I place my hand on his lightly stubbled cheek. "That's good, Jaxon, because I've fallen for you too." I playfully smack his ass and add, "Now get back to fucking me, Mr. Holland."

"Ms. Milne, your wish is my command."

25

BETTER THAN FIGHTING

JAXON

Ah, Cara... I can't get enough of her. If I'm not fucking her, I'm busy tasting her. And when I'm not doing that, I'm touching her in ways I know she loves.

After hours of that kind of loving in the living room, we finally make our way upstairs, where we try out both our beds—first hers, then mine.

We decide we like my bedroom and my bed best, so that's where we fall asleep.

When Cara and I wake up the next morning, rain is pounding heavily onto the roof.

"Hmm," I muse, staring up at the ceiling. "I think any outdoor activities are out for today."

She stretches, nuzzling in close. "Good. I didn't feel like going down to the beach today anyway."

"Mmm…" I kiss her neck. "And why's that?"

She grabs my ass. "Hmm, I think you know."

We start back up where we left off last night, only this time we have a background track of raindrops pelting the roof.

Yeah, staying in is the best.

And so it continues…

We sex it up all day, taking only a few breaks here and there, mainly for bathroom runs. Oh, and one time-out to eat, though for only a small snack.

A little later, after expending so much energy, we decide it's time for a more substantial meal.

"Okay," I say, sitting up in bed. "I'm on it. Though I wish I could stay here with you, sweetheart, and just magically cook something up here."

She purses her lips, those gorgeous lips that have been wrapped around my cock too many times to count today.

"We could always call the housekeeper," she says. "Maybe she could come over and whip up something for us."

"Fuck that," I growl, yanking her to me. "I like being here all alone with you. We can run around naked and fuck everywhere."

"Hmm, you do have a point."

"That's not the only 'point' I have," I murmur, chuckling.

We look down to where my cock is hard again and pointing right at Cara. I'm clearly ready for more, and from the little moan Cara rasps out, I think she is too. But we really need to eat.

"Later?" I raise a brow.

She nods. "Okay, but not too long from now."

Rolling out of bed and throwing on some old sweats, I promise her,

"We'll eat fast."

I then head down to the kitchen to reheat the burgers Cara and I never got to last night. That'll be quick and we can get back to lovin'.

I'm so damn hungry that I end up polishing off three patties as soon as they're ready. Quickly, I plate a burger with all the trimmings for Cara, placing it on a tray so I can take it up to her.

When I push open the bedroom door, she's standing by the bed, fluffing up the pillows. It looks like she's donned one of my shirts, a red and black Wolves' tee. It's huge on her, but damn if she doesn't look adorable, kind of like she's mine.

Ah, I like that.

Possessive me relishes that she's wearing my clothes.

Crawling up onto the bed, and settling back against the newly fluffed pillows, she says, "Mmm, I sure hope that piece of meat is for me."

I look down at my junk, then to the burger.

"Actually, both pieces of meat are for you," I say, snickering.

"Ooh, now you're talking, Jaxon."

I walk over to the bed with the tray. "First, though, I think we'd better get this one in you." I nod down to the burger. "Wouldn't want you passing out from lack of food when we get to dessert, eh?"

She feigns horror. "Good God, no, that'd be awful."

I take a seat on the edge of the bed and turn to her. When she notices that there's only one burger on the plate, she asks, "You already ate?"

"I did," I admit. "And I'm sorry. I just couldn't wait. I was so fucking famished."

Smugly, she retorts, "So you're saying that I wore you out and you needed more fuel?"

"Yes, but it was only temporary. I already feel my energy returning."

Nodding to the tray, she says, "Then I guess you better hand me that burger so I can recharge too."

"You got it, babe."

I place the big burger in front of her and playfully make a sweeping motion over the tray. "Dinner is served, m'lady."

Quietly, and in a most serious tone, she says, "You're so sweet to me, Jaxon."

"Ha, you ain't seen nothin' yet," I assure her as I scoot closer. "You're about to see really sweet Jaxon come out when I feed you each and every bite of this meal."

She looks worried. "Wait. You want to feed me a messy burger?"

It's a big, juicy patty on a bun, stuffed with tomatoes, lettuce, and a squirt of ketchup. It could get messy.

Still, I insist, "I am."

"Well, this should be interesting."

"Don't worry, I came prepared." I produce the fork and knife I've been hiding behind my back this whole time, along with some paper napkins.

Cara laughs. "Jaxon, I swear you think of everything."

I lean over, pressing my lips to hers and murmuring, "I try to, babe."

I then feed Cara each and every bite of that burger. And guess what? There's no mess, which is good, seeing as she *is* wearing my favorite Wolves' tee.

Afterward, she tells me that I'm too good to her. And I tell her that it's only because she deserves the very best.

And she does.

That's why, a short while later, as I'm peeling off that favorite tee of mine from her gorgeous body, I start showing her for the umpteenth time *my* very best.

Later, as she's nestled in my strong, capable arms, she lets out a contented sigh.

"Care to share what you're thinking?" I murmur against the top of her head.

Leaning back and peering up at me, a smile in her hazel eyes, she says, "I was just thinking how amazing this is."

I cock my head. "How do you mean?"

"I mean, this...us." She motions to our intertwined bodies. "Do you realize that we haven't fought once in the past twenty-four hours?"

I think about it and say, "Wow, you're absolutely right. That has to be a record for us."

"I'd say so."

We're quiet then, reflective. I am, at least. I'm thinking about how getting along with Cara is so much nicer than battling with her. I thought battling was better, but that was only because we needed an outlet.

Now we have sex.

I share that with her, and she laughs.

"So," she begins, "are you saying that when we're having sex, we're in another truce of sorts?"

"Yeah, but this one's way better than any before."

"How so, Jaxon?"

I gesture down to our bare bodies. "Well, I'd say it's because sex truces are naked truces."

"Ooh, those are the best."

I caress her cheek. "They are, sweetheart. They really are."

"Mmm..." She stretches out on top of me. "Getting along *is* nice."

"Yeah, good thing I knew all along you'd give in eventually."

Even though I'm totally teasing, she sits up on top of me and smacks me in the chest.

"Jaxon!"

"Ouch." I make a show of playing up that I'm injured, rubbing my pec for effect. "Damn, that hurt, woman."

Cara rolls her eyes. "Yeah, sure it did."

"It did," I insist. "In fact, you should probably kiss it and make it better."

I waggle my eyebrows, and she gets the hint immediately.

"Hmm, yes, maybe I should."

Leaning down, she presses her lips to one pec, then the other.

"Better?" she asks.

"Not yet."

My abs garner her attention next.

"How about now?" she queries in between kisses.

"Better, but..." I slide the sheet down an inch. "Maybe you should focus a little lower."

One kiss to below my belly button and then, peering up at me, eyes hooded with lust, she asks, "Lower still?"

I shrug. "It couldn't hurt."

Cara continues her descent until she runs into something hard and demanding.

"Ah," she says, "I think this particular appendage, huge as it is"—*that's my girl*—"may require more than just kissing."

"What do you suggest?" I rasp, my voice growing thick and rough as lust clouds everything.

"I'm thinking a more intensive treatment, like this…" Cara takes me in her mouth and I let out a groan of pure pleasure.

Yep, getting along is waaay better than fighting.

26

REGRETS, I HAVE A FEW

CARA

Jaxon and I really need to take a break—one that lasts for more than ten minutes—from sexing it up. We've been inside the beach house for two full days, together the whole time.

And still no bickering!

This has to be a record.

I'd like to see if it continues outside the bedroom.

The rain has lasted as long as we've been in the bed. But it seems to finally be tapering off. Outdoors may be an option.

"I don't hear any storming," I say to Jaxon as I cup my hand around my ear and listen for pounding on the roof.

"Nope," he says, "me neither."

We're still in bed, so I snuggle in close to him. "Do you think we should leave this room, then?"

"I did leave," he replies. "Ten minutes ago when I had to pee."

I push his shoulder. "I mean for more than just bathroom breaks, silly man. There is more to life than sex, you know."

He looks appalled. "Hush your mouth, woman."

"Be serious, Jaxon."

"Okay, okay. What did you have in mind?"

"How do you know I have something in mind?" I query.

"'Cause I know you, Cara."

I realize then that he does. He really *knows* me. We aren't two people who just hopped into bed. We've lived together on the island for weeks. And yes, there has been lots of bickering, but maybe Jaxon was right all along when he said it was all just foreplay.

"Cara?" he questions. "Are you still with me?"

"Yes, yes, of course."

"So what do you want to do?"

"How about we take a walk on the beach, like old times?"

"Old times?" Jaxon laughs. "Our walks on the beach weren't that long ago."

"Yes, but a lot's happened since then."

I nod down to us, naked in bed.

"Good point," he says, chuckling.

Jaxon and I decide that a walk on the beach would be nice, so we both shower and dress. He goes with long shorts and a simple white tee, while I opt for bubblegum-pink shorts and a matching camisole.

After we head down to the living room, hand in hand, Jaxon opens the glass doors to check on the weather.

The rain has indeed stopped, but it's super muggy out. So we decide to forgo the walk.

"What do you want to do instead?" Jaxon asks.

I plop down on the sofa, curling my legs up under me. "I don't really have any other ideas," I confess. "It's not like we have a TV to watch or anything."

"True, but we do have my laptop and your tablet. We could watch something on either of those."

I think it over and conclude, "Okay, but I think your laptop would work better since it's bigger. What do you want to watch?"

He walks over to retrieve his laptop from a side table and then sits down beside me on the sofa.

"Well, I've been meaning to get around to watching the final Stanley Cup game. Would you be up for that?"

Brow knitting, I say, "Wait, you haven't watched it yet? That game's been up online for weeks."

"I know," Jaxon sighs. "I just…couldn't. Not until now."

I'm totally confused, so I ask, "What changed?"

He takes my hand. "You, sweetheart, *you're* what changed in my life." He turns me to him and releases my hand so he can cup my cheek.

Oh my God, the emotion in his beautiful emerald eyes. It's like I'm freaking sunshine—*his* sunshine.

And sure enough, the next words out of his mouth are, "You make me feel like I can do anything, Cara. Take on the world, even."

I swallow hard.

Jesus, he couldn't watch the game because of *me*, though he doesn't know that. And now he *can* watch it because of me.

What a mess.

If Jaxon knew that I'm Mr. Hockeypants, he wouldn't be so quick to say I make him feel like he can take on the world.

I wouldn't be his sunshine, either. I'd be more like the fucking hurricane that wrecked his life.

I should tell him. I better just do it now...before we get in any deeper.

Crap, this is what happens when you go with your heart, not your head. You forget that you have to deal with the consequences of those not-so-thought-out actions later.

Still, I have no regrets; I can just fix things now.

I open my mouth, ready to confess everything, but nothing comes out.

My mouth snaps shut.

I'm still so damn afraid. No, now is worse. I'm freaking terrified, more than ever before. Now that we've slept together, if he has a poor reaction to the news my heart will be crushed.

Crap, I should've told him first. But there was no time. Now I'm scared to death that we'll end before we even really begin. This is so new and so fresh. Can a burgeoning relationship like ours withstand a hit like that?

I just don't know.

Jaxon Holland has turned my world upside down, and I like where I've landed. He's blurred the lines between love and hate and smudged up my heart.

But it's not so smudged up that I can't see what emotion has won—love.

Oh my God—I *love* Jaxon Holland.

Like for real.

I'm not simply falling. I freaking fell.

Shit, well that settles it. I absolutely must fess up about my blog... eventually.

But today, right now, I want this little reprieve.

Can I at least have that?

In case it does all end.

Yes, yes you can.

"Cara?" Jaxon's peering at me with great concern. "Are you all right?"

I wave my hand around like I'm swishing away a nagging fly. This dilemma of mine is exactly that. I'm dealing with a pesky guilty conscience.

"I'm fine," I say.

He tilts his head. "Are you sure?"

"Yes, I'm sure." I pat his hand. "Now let's watch the game."

STANLEY CUP BLUES

JAXON

Watching the game is hard, even with Cara by my side. I feel awful since it should've been the Wolves playing the Devils for hockey superiority.

Alas, it's all water under the bridge now. Or ice, as the case may be.

Yeah right. If only. Nothing can take away the pain of fucking up in that elimination game.

Uttering one long-ass sigh, I continue watching.

And it's brutal.

It's the seventh game of the series, winner takes all. The Oilers are looking good. Still, I can't help but think how the Wolves could've taken the Devils in four.

We'll never know since I screwed up. And I bear that weight on my shoulders like Atlas holding up the world. I feel it even now, so much so that I feel the urge to hop up from the sofa.

So I do. And the laptop slides over to Cara's lap as I stand abruptly.

"Sorry," I mutter. I begin to pace. "I just need to walk around a little bit."

She presses Pause on the game and places the laptop on the coffee table. "Should we watch the rest another time?"

"No, just give me a minute."

"Jaxon," she breathes out. "You know that playoff loss in round two wasn't your fault, right?"

I laugh bitterly. "Try telling that to the fans."

When I glance over at her, she looks really...guilty?

Huh?

Why would Cara feel responsible in any way? She's not the one who zoned out and messed up crucial plays. She's not the one who got called for a penalty at the end. She's not the one who lost the game.

That's why it's perplexing when she lowers her head and murmurs what can only be described as a heartfelt, "I am so, so sorry, Jaxon."

I drop back down beside her so I can drape an arm over her shoulders. "Hey, hey, it's not your fault, Cara."

"I kind of feel like it is, though," she inexplicably replies.

Wow, we sure must have some connection. She feels what *I* feel? This is incredible.

"You really are the girl for me," I murmur as I begin nuzzling her neck.

She jolts away. "How can you even say something like that, Jaxon?"

Yeesh, she's taking the Wolves loss harder than I am. *Crazy.*

"How can I not?" I counter, leaning back against the cushions. "We're growing so close that you actually feel my pain."

She winces. "Oh, Jaxon..."

"Not to worry, sweetheart. I'm going to take it to heart what you just said. The loss wasn't entirely my fault."

"It really wasn't," she mumbles, shaking her head.

"Hey, tell you what. I'll stop blaming myself if you can smile for me."

She gives me her best attempt, but it's a weak one.

"Come on, Cara. You can do better than that."

It takes a few more tries, along with me cracking some really stupid jokes, but I finally get her to smile.

It's not the biggest grin, but it's genuine, so I'll take it.

Still, somewhere deep inside of me, I feel like I'm missing something here.

I just have no idea what it could be.

28

A CAKE TO BAKE

CARA

Oh my God, I feel like the world's biggest jerk. Watching Jaxon's torment is pure torture for me.

Because I caused it!

If it hadn't been for Mr. Hockeypants's scathing post, Jaxon's mistakes would've been forgotten long ago. As it stands, the last time I checked, the fans were still bitching and moaning about him online. Not on my blog, of course, since the comments remain turned off, but on many other hockey sites the venomous words are still flying.

When he has to take a break from watching the game, it just about freaking kills me.

I'm glad when he tells me he's finally putting it all behind him. *Phew.* That's the real reason why I can finally smile for him. Though I let him believe it's because of his corny jokes. I'd pretty much do anything for this man right now.

That's why when he asks me if we can talk about some things—after we finally do finish watching the Stanley Cup final, which the Devils win—I'm all in.

"Sure," I say as I sit up straight. "What's on your mind?"

Jaxon closes the laptop and sets it aside.

"I know we have a few more weeks left on the island," he begins, "but I've been thinking about how things might play out once we're back in Las Vegas."

Clearly, we're about to have a talk on where we stand. I thought I'd have to be the one to initiate it, but apparently not. I'm glad Jaxon is so forward thinking. It bodes well for our future.

Yeah, wait till he finds out you're Mr. Hockeypants. I doubt that'll bode well for your future.

Enough!

I clear my throat...and my head.

"How would *you* like for things to play out?" I ask.

He nods and seems to ponder. "Well, I obviously want to keep seeing you once we're back in Vegas. I kind of already figured, even with all of our bickering"—we share a smile—"that we'd stay in touch. But now that we're much more than just friends, it's a given."

"It is," I happily agree.

"So..." He blows out a breath. "I have to warn you, I'm a little rusty when it comes to relationships—"

"As am I," I interject truthfully.

"I guess what I'm trying to say is, do you consider us to be exclusive?"

Is he kidding?

Yes! I almost yell out.

But I should at least *try* to play it cool, right?

Coyly, I lift a brow. "Do *you* want us to be exclusive, Jaxon?"

"Hell, yeah," he blurts out.

Hmm, so much for playing it cool.

He's not playing games, so why should I?

I drop the coy façade and breathe out, "Thank goodness. I was hoping you'd say that."

"Shit, babe, the thought of you with some other man would totally destroy me."

"Same here," I say. But then I think it over and amend, "I mean, the thought of you with another woman. That would totally destroy me." I ponder some more and add, "Though you out with a man would definitely upset me too."

That makes Jaxon laugh.

Folding me into his arms, he assures me, "No men, babe, I promise."

I narrow my eyes up at him. "What about other women?"

"None of them, either. It's just you and me, babe."

"Isn't that a song, Jaxon?"

"I don't know. But it can be. It can be our song, eh?"

I smile contentedly. "That sounds perfect."

I lean into him and everything just feels so right.

I only hope it will remain like this once I come clean.

The next week on the island is our best yet. Jaxon and I have so much fun. We hang out on the beach during the days, like before, but the nights are so much better. We still take long walks, but when we come back to the house, we make love all night.

As a result, I grow to love him more and more. I think he loves me too—I see it in his eyes, feel it in his touch. He said he was falling, right? Well, maybe he's fully fallen.

Everything is just so relaxed with us, so different than before. Some days we just chill out on the patio. Those are the times we like to watch the little lizards run and play, making me remember how Jaxon saved one on that fateful day that finally brought us together.

The kindness he showed made me fall for him completely. And I've been trying to think of a way to show him some sort of kindness in return, like a gesture of some sort.

So when I learn that today is his twenty-fourth birthday, I know this is my chance. He won't have any idea that I know, seeing as he hasn't said anything about it being his big day today.

Good. I can totally surprise him.

I knew surreptitiously checking hockey blogs this fine morning, while he's in the shower, was a good move. That's how I came upon the info about it being his birthday today.

But now I think he's coming out of the bathroom, so I power down the tablet and set it aside.

On a side note, I have to say it was good to see the vitriol against Jaxon has finally died down. That means I should be able to tell him about Mr. Hockeypants real soon. And maybe I'll luck out and he won't be all that angry after all.

Still, I'm not going to bring it up today. Not on his birthday, no way.

What I do plan to do is bake him a cake…and then serve it to him in the nude. I'm committed to making this his best birthday ever, and that's a good start. Plus, it's my "kind" gesture—hee-hee.

First, though, I need to figure out a way to keep him out of the house for a few hours.

Hmmm…

We start the day like usual, with breakfast downstairs. Most days Jaxon makes the food, since he's a pretty good cook, but today I offer.

I can't let him cook his own birthday breakfast, right?

"Just chill while I make you something delicious," I tell him as I open the fridge. "You're always cooking for me, so it's only fair."

Jaxon holds up his hands as he takes a seat at the breakfast bar. "Hey, you're not about to hear any argument from me."

I just nod since I'm a little distracted.

Peering into the fridge, I'm aghast to discover we're running really low on eggs. This could throw a wrench into my birthday cake-baking plan.

Ack, the housekeeper is due in tomorrow and she's sure to bring more. But I need those eggs for Jaxon's cake today.

Thinking fast, I close the fridge and smile over at Jaxon. "Hey, how does bacon and toast sound for breakfast this morning?"

"Add in a couple of poached eggs and you have yourself a deal," he replies.

Shit, think fast.

"Uh, I'm actually not feeling very egg-y today. I think the smell of them might bother me. Do you mind if we just skip the eggs?"

Jaxon stares at me in confusion. "But you usually enjoy having eggs for breakfast."

"I know." I make a face and a big show of rubbing my stomach. "Not this morning, though. Like I said, I'm feeling a little off."

"You sure you're okay, Cara?"

"I'll be fine in a few. You know how I sometimes feel icky in the morning." That part is true. "I'm sure I'll be back to normal in a couple of hours."

"Okay," he says, sighing. "No eggs, then."

Poor Jaxon. I hate making up such an elaborate tale. Not to mention withholding his beloved eggs. I like eggs, yes, but Jaxon freaking loves them. Remember the one he put in the smoothie? So yeah...

Still, his cake is the priority. Therefore, toast and bacon it is.

After breakfast, we make our way out to the beach.

As I settle onto a lounge chair, I notice Jaxon is peering over at me curiously.

"Your boobs look bigger," he remarks.

I glance down at my chest. "It's just an illusion," I explain. "This new bikini has a push-up bra sewn into it."

It's true. I ordered a bright orange bikini a while ago and it finally arrived. One of the selling points was that it creates "amazing" cleavage.

I have to agree.

And so apparently does Jaxon.

Yanking me over to his chaise lounge, eliciting a squeal of delight from me, he slides his hand down into the top.

"Fuck, Cara," he rasps as he plies seductively at one nipple, then the other, making them pebble under his skilled touch. "I want you so badly right now."

Since it's his birthday, although I can't let him know that I know that just yet, I'm all-in on making any wishes of his today come true.

I sit up and straddle his lap. Jaxon sighs and peels down the bikini top, but he doesn't take it off all the way. With even more of a push-up effect now, my boobs look *huge*.

Jaxon groans and rubs his smooth, freshly shaved face on each before he finally claims one nipple with his mouth.

While he sucks, licks, and nibbles, I help him shimmy his swim trunks down a little. His cock springs free, hard and erect, and I see and want.

Oh, do I want.

Groaning, I push aside my bikini bottoms so he can just slip up into me.

When he does, I gasp, "Yes, Jaxon, yes."

We take turns, me bouncing up and down on his length and him pumping up into me. Under the blazing sun, with sweat pouring down our slick bodies, and the waves crashing beyond us, we grind and thrust and just fuck the hell out of each other. We are one man and one woman on this isolated island.

Good thing for that, as I wouldn't want an audience for this carnal show.

Afterward, Jaxon and I swim and frolic in the ocean, washing away the physical evidence, but not the lasting feelings of attachment, from our lusty encounter.

When we return to our chairs, I wait till the sun dries my skin a bit, and then I say, "I think I'm going to go inside for a while."

He lowers his sunglasses, his green eyes so vivid and bright in the sun. "Is everything okay?"

"Yes, yes." Jumping up, I lean down to kiss him. "Everything is better than okay. But I have something I need to do. Are you cool with hanging out here for a little while by yourself? I promise it'll be worth it."

Oops, that last bit just slipped out. All the sex and the sun have clearly muddled my mind. I just hope I didn't tip him off that I'm aware it's his birthday.

Jaxon *must* think I'm up to something else, though, seeing as he doesn't question me or argue.

Wow, that's kind of shocking. Bickering used to be our go-to interaction. How things have changed.

"No problem, babe." He smacks my ass playfully. "Go do whatever it is you have to do. I'll be fine out here."

I scamper off before he changes his mind and decides to come with me.

We can't have that, as someone has a cake to bake.

29

NAKED BIRTHDAYS ARE THE BEST

JAXON

I don't know what Cara is up to, not exactly, but I have a feeling it has to do with my birthday.

She must've found out that it's today.

Maybe since she's been taking a bigger interest in hockey—thanks to my influence, of course—she checked up on me online and found the info.

I'm pleased she's taking such an interest, but I sure hope she doesn't run across any additional Mr. Hockeypants bullshit. It was bad enough that day she was looking at his site. I caught her red-handed, but I think she's done with him. She's on to bigger and better blogs these days, I'm sure.

She checks her tablet every morning, I know that. Hell, I've caught her slipping it under the bed or onto the side table a number of times.

I chuckle to myself. I swear one of these days I'm going to sneak a peek to see which hockey-related pages she frequents these days. If she's wasting her time on any crappy shit—like Mr. Fuckface's blog—I'll be sure to redirect her to more reputable sites.

In any case, she must've checked a good one this morning.

No, make that a great one if it provided her with the date of my birth.

Ah, and what a day it's already been—the breakfast she made and then the sex on the beach.

Yes, it is indeed a good life.

I lean back and relax, knowing I'll be out here for a while. I need to give Cara plenty of time to do whatever it is she's up to.

Later, when it gets too hot down on the beach, I move up to the patio. There's shade on one side, so I drag a lounge chair over there.

And that's when I start to nod off.

I dream the best shit, I swear. Stuff about Cara and me once we return to Las Vegas. I dream she comes to my games all the time and cheers me on like great girlfriends do. I dream of introducing her to my friends and teammates. I've always suspected that she'd get along beautifully with the wives and girlfriends, and in my dream everyone adores her. It's funny too, as the guys are shocked that I'm in a relationship.

And that I'm so in love.

I wake up immediately at that part.

Whoa, what? What the fuck was that?

I realize then that I'm in love with Cara Milne.

And if my dream is any kind of premonition, we have a wonderful future ahead of us.

Whoa, this is amazing. I don't feel anxious or trapped, not like how

I used to feel when I'd be getting in deep with someone. Those were the times when I'd usually end things.

But, fuck, I can't imagine doing that with Cara.

I can think of absolutely no reason to not move forward with her. I mean, shit, we're so open and honest with each other. And I just feel so overall good about her.

Check that, I feel great!

My elation is amped even higher when I step into the house about an hour later and Cara emerges from the kitchen with a huge triple-layer chocolate cake. Candles flicker in the breeze, but that doesn't stop her. She smiles, before she breaks into a super-sexy rendition of "Happy Birthday."

And I'm not joking when I say super-sexy, seeing as she's completely naked.

I have to chuckle. It may be *my* birthday, but she's the one in her birthday suit.

"Sweetheart, you are the absolute best girlfriend in the world," I declare.

Finishing the song, she sets the cake down carefully on the coffee table.

"Thank you, Jaxon. But you better make your wish before the candles melt into the icing."

"I would make one," I say, "but I think all my wishes have already come true."

"Oh, come on," she urges, her bare body glorious as she stands there bathed in the glow of the candles. "I'm sure you can think of *something* to wish for, something unrelated to us."

"That's hard," I confess.

She gestures to the semi now tenting my swim trunks and coyly replies, "It looks like something else is hard too."

"Well, you are standing there with nothing on, gorgeous."

Stepping over to me, she smacks my arm. "Stop stalling and make that wish."

"Okay, okay." I ponder and ponder, and finally come up with something. "I wish for the Wolves to win another Stanley Cup."

"You guys will," she murmurs softly.

"From your lips to all the hockey gods' ears," I say.

And then I blow out all the candles, which makes Cara jump up and down.

That, of course, makes her perky breasts bounce.

Fuck, I can never get enough of her.

I have to look away, or she's going to be lying flat on the floor in a hot minute with me buried deep inside her.

I lock my eyes on her hands—that's safe—as she cuts us each a piece of cake. But it's not safe for long when she announces that I have to be naked too.

"It's only fair, Jaxon," she coos.

"Hell, I'm in." I start disrobing immediately. "I'm liking this naked birthday theme."

"Ha, you're going to like naked birthdays even more in about a minute. I'm not done yet."

I have no idea what that means, but I find out soon enough when I take my first delectable bite of cake.

That's when Cara drops to her knees in front of me.

"Fuck, babe, whatcha doing?" I ask.

"Oh, just this…" She dips her finger into the icing from her slice of cake and deposits a fat glob on the tip of my now fully erect cock.

"Shit." My dick twitches in anticipation as she starts licking off the icing. "Fuuuck."

Naked birthdays, like naked truces, are awesome.

30

LOVE IS IN THE AIR

CARA

Jaxon *loves* his birthday. He tells me so again and again. The cake, the sexing in the sun, staying naked for the rest of the day, and of course me licking icing off his dick, not just once but again and again, all made his day.

"So when is *your* birthday, Cara?" he asks as we're lounging around in bed.

"September 16th," I murmur, my cheek resting against his smooth, firm chest. "I turn twenty-three this year."

"Hmm, so you're a year younger than me."

"Yes, I am, you cradle robber," I tease.

"What ever you say, old man chaser," he lobs back.

"Oh, stop. My birthday is only a year and two months after yours. And hey"—I lift up my head and peer up at him—"I just thought of something interesting."

"What's that?" he asks.

"Our birthdays are exactly two months apart. Yours is July 16th and mine is September 16th."

He wistfully twirls a lock of my hair around his finger. "Huh, that is pretty cool. But another cool thing is that your birthday will fall on the day after the Wolves' first preseason game this year."

"No way," I say. "That's wild."

"Not wild, babe, more like perfect. It means I'll only have a light practice the morning of your birthday."

As I lazily trace imaginary hearts on his chest, I murmur, "So that means we'll have the whole day to celebrate?"

"It does indeed." He smiles down at me wickedly. "And the whole night."

"Hmm…" I trace a little lower. "I like the sound of that even more."

Brows suddenly furrowing, he says, "I gotta tell you, though, the pressure is on."

I still my hand, flattening my palm against his hard abs. His skin is so deliciously warm.

"How do you mean?" I ask.

"Well, it'll be *my* turn to make *your* birthday as special as you've made mine."

I'm happy that's he's happy, and I tell him so. It warms my heart that his birthday was a success. Plus, I love how good it feels to discuss how things will be once we're back home. It makes our summer romance on this island feel so much more real.

I sigh, content that Jaxon and I are truly together. We're doing this, by God!

We're a couple and we're in love.

That's the moment I realize I *have* to tell him. Not about the blog. There'll be time for that later. This is far more pressing. We've told each other that we're falling, but we've never said the actual words "I love you."

It's time to change that.

Peering up at Jaxon, I lay my heart on the line.

"Jaxon Holland, I have to tell you something important."

"What's that, babe?"

"I love you. I love you very much, in fact."

His brows shoot up, but he appears really pleased to hear this.

And then he says, "I love you too, Cara," and I'm more than happy. I'm ecstatic.

This is real, and we're going to make it work. Here on the island and in Nevada, our love will transcend any place, any time, and any problem.

Yep, it'll all work out just fine.

Time flies by swiftly, and soon there's only a week left until we're to leave the island and return to the desert.

August is nearly upon us, and Jaxon wants to return soon in order to start a more regimented preseason workout.

Running, doing sit-ups, and rocking out a couple hundred push-ups every morning is great and all, but he needs to hit the ice.

"I'm starting to really miss it," he shares with me one evening when we're chilling out on the patio.

"What do you mean?" I ask, glancing over at him. "Are you saying you miss the actual *ice*?"

"Yes, and don't you dare laugh."

"Um, I'm not."

But I so am.

I try to compose myself when he adds in an über serious voice, "Hockey is in my heart and soul, Cara. And the ice is a big part of that."

"Well, I think that's sweet," I say. I get it, but I feel compelled to add, "So long as there's room in there somewhere for me, I'm cool with that."

I reach for his hand, but he leans over instead and plants a kiss on my cheek.

"Always, my love," he whispers. "There will always be a huge part of my heart *and* my soul reserved strictly for you."

"Aw, you're such a sweetheart, Jaxon."

He glances around, pretending to be worried. "Shh, don't let that get out."

"Don't worry," I whisper, playing along. "It'll stay between us."

We grow quiet then, and for this really long while we just hold hands and watch the sun as it melts into the ocean.

As the waves and sand are painted in shades of red, orange, and pink, I remark, "God, it's so beautiful here. I'm going to miss this place so much."

Jaxon squeezes my hand. "I know what you mean. I'll miss it too. But we'll make new, great memories in Vegas, sweetheart. And we'll always have this summer to look back on."

"True," I agree. "But I love how it's just you and me here."

"I do too. But you know what? Maybe Noel will play in another world championship next year and we can come back."

"That'd be nice," I say. And then, out of curiosity, I ask, "Speaking of the world championships, those ended over a month ago, right?"

"Yes," he confirms.

"Then why is Noel still in Europe? His sister mentioned in an email that he's still in Sweden. I forgot to ask why when I wrote her back, though."

Jaxon shrugs. "I'm not sure, either. I haven't talked to Noel in a while. Who knows? Maybe he met someone and fell in love."

That makes me smile. "Like we did?"

"Yes, babe, like us." Our eyes meet and I sigh contentedly.

We spend more time outside, just laughing and talking the evening away. Eventually, though, I can't stop yawning.

"Oh my goodness, I am so sorry, Jaxon. Guess I'm sleepier than I realized."

Gesturing to the house, he says, "If you want to head in to bed, I'm cool with that. I'll be up soon myself. I just want to spend a few more minutes out here."

"Okay." I nod. "I'll see you inside."

I am really tired and practically have to drag myself upstairs. But then I get a second wind.

Weird how those happen, huh?

Shaking my head and wondering why the brain turns on when you want it to turn off, I detour to my old bedroom so I can check email. I left my tablet in there earlier when I was changing into a pair of shorts.

Maybe if I do a few mundane things I'll feel sleepy again.

Crawling onto my old bed, I sit cross-legged as I power on my tablet. To my chagrin, I only have one email. It's from Noelle, filling me in on the latest and greatest with her internship—she still loves it like crazy but is annoyed that it's cutting into her social life. She also writes how she better hear from me soon or she's sending in a rescue team.

That makes me laugh, and I grab my phone so I can shoot her a quick text.

Hey, no rescue teams, I type. *I'm alive and well.*

I hit Send and she replies immediately. We then send texts back and forth rapid-fire for about five minutes. It's all fun, light topics until she mentions that she's feeling blue.

Aw, don't be sad, I text. *You know I love you.*

I know. And I'm trying not to, but between you being gone and these long hours, I feel like an old cat lady.

But you don't even have a cat, I text, laughing.

True.

I promise her then that we can hit the town like old times once I'm back in Vegas.

But I won't be looking for love, I add.

She knows all about my new relationship with Jaxon. Not that she's surprised. She called it from the start, remember?

Once we finally wrap up, I slide my phone onto the nightstand. But I'm still feeling pretty awake, so I pick up the tablet and start visiting a bunch of hockey sites.

That's when I learn I missed a few key off-season trades today. One in particular was a big trade the Wolves made.

Hmmm...

I look over at the closed door and bite my lip. I really should log on and compose a post about this. I probably have time to do it too. This is big, and the fans will be looking for a Mr. Hockeypants reaction. I mean, hell, the Wolves have traded right winger Drew Chidders! That's a really big deal.

I've always heard, though, that he's a real asshole. Not to mention that he did nothing in the playoffs.

In my opinion, it's no real loss. And that means that's what Mr.

Hockeypants thinks too.

I glance again at the door.

Man, I'd love to get these thoughts down in a post.

But do I have time before Jaxon comes upstairs?

I don't know.

I think about it some more...

Can I write a short blog post, addressing the Wolves trade, in, like, under ten minutes?

I nod. Yeah, I think so. Though that doesn't mean my heart isn't racing and my palms aren't sweaty as I prepare to do so.

Damn, this is crazy. I really need to let Jaxon know I'm Mr. Hockeypants.

First, though, I'd like to make a few key changes to the blog. I've been thinking a lot lately. After things spun out of control with the Jaxon post, I've learned a lot.

One is that I need to be more careful with my words.

That's why I'm considering softening Mr. Hockeypants's rough edges and harsh language. He can still be snarky and hard-hitting, and he'll certainly still curse like a sailor, but there should be no more personal attacks. They're just too damaging. I've seen the harm careless words can cause.

Sighing heavily, I start typing.

I'm careful to keep the tone positive, writing only glowing things about the new guy we picked up. I even refrain from ripping on the departing Chidders. Though if anyone deserves a good blasting, it's him.

Just as I'm finishing, I hear Jaxon coming in downstairs.

Eek, better get this up fast.

I hit Publish at the same instant Jaxon is knocking on the bedroom door.

"Babe, why are you in your old bedroom?" he asks, sounding perplexed. "I thought you said you were exhausted and going to bed? And why's the door closed?"

With lightning speed, I toss the tablet under the bed.

"Come on in," I call out. "It's unlocked."

The door opens and he steps in.

"I guess I just closed it out of habit," I rush to explain, shrugging.

Like that doesn't sound shady.

"Mmm, okay," he murmurs, glancing around.

Thank God my guy is a pervert. He's not glancing around with suspicion. Nope, there's nothing but mischievousness in his eyes, especially when they settle in on me.

"You know what?" He grins, and I know that look. Oh, do I know that look. "I just had the most brilliant idea, Cara."

This is a far more preferable turn in events, so I roll with it, promptly forgetting about blog posts and the tablet under the bed.

"Why, do share," I purr.

Eyes glinting playfully, he says, "I was thinking about how we've never actually *slept* in here. And you have that nice big bed." He nods to the king-size monstrosity I'm seated in the middle of. "Why don't we stay in here tonight? Plus, we can christen the mattress."

I remind him that not only is his bed the exact same size as mine, but that we "christened" *both* beds before we decided to stay in his room.

He snickers. "That's right. Good times."

He mentions a few of the things we did in my bed and how he'd like to repeat them.

"You're so bad. Stop. You're getting me all worked up."

"Good." He laughs. "That means my devious plan is working."

I shake my head, loving every second of this.

"You're impossible, Jaxon."

I throw a pillow at him and he catches it easily, and then he comes over to sit on the edge of the bed.

"Seriously, babe, I really do feel like sleeping in here tonight."

"Yeah right, you're not fooling anyone," I snort. "You just want to do all those things you just mentioned in a different bed."

He waggles his brows. "Variety is the spice of life, you know?"

He has a point, so I agree we should stay in my old room for the night.

Of course, we get started right away on rechristening the bed. Jaxon is really into it too and wears me out. That doesn't happen often so I let him gloat about what a man he is.

While he's preening like a stud muffin, I drift off.

31

I CAN'T F*CKING BELIEVE THIS

JAXON

When I wake up early the next morning, Cara is sleeping soundly.

I think I may have really and truly worn her out, no joke. I say her name out loud and nothing.

Oh, well, it is kind of early.

Sighing, I sit up and lean back on the pillows so I can watch the woman I love sleep.

Jesus, it scares me sometimes how into her I am. But I guess this is what real love feels like. It's kind of scary and great all at the same time. Great for all the obvious reasons, but scary knowing that someone holds the power to rip out your heart.

But I shouldn't worry.

Cara is the best.

She'd never hurt me.

I smile as I think of her, and then about last night. Not the sex part, though that was amazing. But no, my thoughts are on how we remained out on the patio long after the sun had set, just talking and feeling close.

Fuck, she's so easy to be around. I can't wait till she meets my teammates. I bet they'll love her as much as I do.

Whoa, wait. Maybe not *love* her love her. The guys on our team are all pretty decent-looking. I don't need that kind of competition. As long as they like her, that'll be good.

Crap, this love stuff sure stirs up the jealousy.

It's all so tiring. I'm feeling exhausted already. Or maybe that's because it's freaking early to be awake.

So why stay up? I should just lie back down and catch a few extra z's along with Cara.

Yeah, that sounds good.

But just as I'm rearranging the pillows, I accidentally knock Cara's phone off the nightstand and it somehow ends up under the bed.

I shake my head. I mean really, what's the freaking chance? I couldn't do that again if I tried.

Leaning over the side of the mattress, I reach underneath the bed, feeling for the phone. But what I run into instead is Cara's tablet. She must've knocked it off the bed or stand last night before I came in, like I just did with her phone. This bed is clearly an electronics eater. Good thing we sleep in my room.

I finally feel her phone under my hand. Grabbing it up, along with the tablet, I set both items on the nightstand.

And that's when Cara's tablet flashes to life.

I should turn that off, so it doesn't lose battery power.

I reach over to do just that, but then something on her screen catches my eye. I guess it's because there's a hockey stick and a puck.

"Aw," I murmur, "how adorable is that. My girl was checking out a hockey site before bedtime. Even I don't always do that."

So many warm and fuzzy feelings wash over me...until I take a closer look and see that the site is none other than that fucking Mr. Hockeypants's blog.

"What the fuck?" I hiss. "Why would she visit his trashy blog again? Didn't we go over this?"

Almost like she subconsciously hears me, Cara murmurs something indecipherable in her sleep. But she doesn't wake up.

Good thing since I'm totally focused on the blog page now.

And why is that?

Because I see it's in some kind of an "administrative editor" mode.

What the hell is this shit? How could Cara have access like that to someone else's blog?

I scroll down, my heart racing.

It looks like this "administrative editor" published a post last night, right about the time I arrived upstairs.

Shit, no.

For this one long, drawn-out minute or so, time seems to stop. I just don't want to face the truth staring me in the face. I'd rather believe Cara is a hacker, and she's hacked into Mr. Hockeypants's blog to delete the whole damn thing.

But nothing's been deleted.

Hell, there's a new fucking post.

With my heart hammering in my chest, I read the post and discover it's about the recent Wolves trade. The thing that strikes me is that it's not only well-written, but it's been penned by someone who definitely knows hockey.

"But Cara knows hardly anything about the sport," I whisper, feeling kind of dazed, and definitely betrayed. "Or so I thought."

I can't believe this is fucking happening.

I guess I can call off my investigating attorney.

I know the truth now—Cara is Mr. Hockeypants.

I'm stunned…and about a lot.

Not just that this is her secret identity, *her* fucking blog. But what about the other stuff?

The things she wrote about me, it hurts my heart.

And she's been lying all along about her hockey knowledge. She's always known more.

Hell, she's one of the biggest hockey bloggers around, for fuck's sake. Mr. Hockeypants is known for his…her…*whatever* expertise on the sport.

I look over at a woman I clearly don't know at all and shake my head.

I just can't even.

"Who are you?" I whisper. "Because you're definitely not the person I thought you were."

I feel sick, I feel betrayed, I feel like a damn fucking fool. Why would she keep all this from me?

Has everything that's happened on the island been a lie?

Does she even fucking love me at all?

And that's when my heart fissures open.

I know then that there's only one thing left to do—get the hell away from Cara Milne.

Or whoever the hell she is.

32

MR. HOCKEYPANTS REVEALED

CARA

I wake up from the most restful sleep. But when I roll over, expecting to find Jaxon sleeping peacefully next to me, he's not there.

Huh?

The space next to me is not only vacant but it's cool, meaning he's been gone for a while.

It's weird that Jaxon is up so early. He usually lounges around in bed with me on lazy mornings like this, especially after nights like the one we just had.

Thinking maybe he's close by, I stretch out and say rather loudly, "God, I love that man. And I sure do wish he were here so I could show him."

I'm hoping maybe he'll hear me and come back to bed.

But alas, crickets.

Oh, well.

I roll out of bed, slip on a short silky robe, and head downstairs, expecting to find Jaxon in the kitchen, probably making us breakfast.

But he's not there either.

"Jaxon, are you around?" I call out.

Again, no response.

This is really weird.

A strange sense of dread washes over me, like something bad is up.

Carefully, I walk into the living room and notice that the sliding glass doors leading out to the patio are securely closed. That means Jaxon's not down on the beach, nor is he out on the patio. We almost always leave the doors slightly ajar when we're out.

I purse my lips and look around, and that's when I notice two big bags over by the front door. They're not just any bags, either; they're suitcases that belong to Jaxon. I remember them from day one when he left them in the very same spot.

What the hell is going on?

Where is Jaxon? And, more importantly, what's with the bags? Where is he going?

Neither of us is set to leave for another week or so. It's so up in the air, we don't even have airline tickets booked yet.

So what is this all about?

Suddenly, the front door swings open and Jaxon walks in. His phone is up to his ear and he's obviously preoccupied. He doesn't even see me, despite the fact I'm standing in the middle of the living room.

As he bends down and starts messing with his bags, I hear him saying to whoever's on the other end, "Yes, and I need a ride to the airport as soon as possible."

Why does he need to go to the airport?

I wonder if some sort of an emergency has come up back in Nevada. If so, why wouldn't he have woken me up and told me so? I'd go with him. We're together now, we're a team. This is what couples do.

I suddenly have an overriding sense of dread that he hasn't told me because this is about me.

But what did I do? I've been sleeping, for fuck's sake. And things were fine last night, better than fine even.

"Jaxon," I croak. "What's going on?"

He spins around, his face an inscrutable mask.

Lowering the phone, he slips it into his jeans pocket.

Crossing his arms over his wide chest, the black material of his tee growing taut, he snipes, "Finally up, eh?"

I start to walk toward him but stop cold when he narrows his eyes at me. I've never seen his emerald greens so stormy...nor so tortured.

"What in the hell is happening?" I cry out.

"I'm leaving," he says flatly.

"B-but why? Did something happen? Did I do something to upset you?"

He scoffs, "Ha. That may be the biggest understatement of this whole summer. Did you do something to upset me?" He laughs derisively. "I'd say yes the fuck so."

Uncrossing his arms and reaching over to a stand by the door, he grabs something I didn't see before—a tablet, *my* tablet.

And I know for a fact I didn't leave it there.

Shit!

It all becomes clear then—he saw the blog post and suspects, rightly so, that I wrote it.

He knows I'm Mr. Hockeypants.

Fuck my life.

He wasn't supposed to find out like this. I should have told him sooner.

And how could I have been so stupid last night?

I never powered down the tablet, I just slid it under the bed. Jaxon clearly found it there. And once it came to life, which it would have simply from someone tapping the screen, or even touching it inadvertently, the last page would pop up—the "administrative editor" mode of my Mr. Hockeypants blog, after I had finished writing and publishing my post.

"Fuck."

"Fuck is right," Jaxon snaps.

He turns the tablet my way so I can see the incriminating blog page and the mode it's in.

"*You're* that fucking Hockeypants dude?" he bellows.

"I am," I confess, eyes flittering to anywhere but landing on him.

"Don't look away from me," he spits out.

He's so angry. I knew this would happen. That's why I lived in a bubble of denial, why I kept the truth from him. I would've told him eventually, but would it have gone any better than him finding out on his own?

I don't think so, not anymore.

This was always a no-win situation for me.

And, really, it was for him too.

I sigh, and Jaxon's anger dissipates to something far worse—hurt and confusion.

It tears my heart in two when he murmurs dejectedly, "But you're not even a dude. I always thought he was a guy. I mean, the blog's called Mr. Hockeypants, right? Why not name it Miss Hockeypants…or Ms.

Hockeypants?"

I shake my head and answer him truthfully. "I don't know. The name just kind of came to me one day."

Angry Jaxon returns, like he's just gotten hold of himself.

Disgusted, he murmurs, "It doesn't matter."

"But—"

"But nothing, Cara." Tossing the tablet back onto the stand with an angry clatter, he says dryly, "I really don't care…about the blog…about you…about any fucking thing."

"Come on, you don't mean that," I quietly state, trying to sound soothing. "Just let me explain."

Racing over to him, I try to touch his arm, but he jerks away like I'm attempting to burn him.

Shaking his head, he says, "No, Cara. Just leave me alone. I'm out of here. I booked a flight back to Las Vegas, and there's a ride on the way to take me to the airport. It should be here any minute."

He slides his sunglasses on and begins fumbling with his bags again, preparing to go.

No, no, no.

I want to grab him, hold him, and apologize over and over again. But I have to respect that he needs space. So, reluctantly, I back away.

Still, I have to try.

"Jaxon, can we please talk about this?"

He looks up from his bags and laughs bitterly. "What's there to say? I think the facts are pretty clear. You've been lying to me this whole summer about what you knew about hockey and, more importantly"— his voice rises—"about who the fuck you really are!"

"That's why I lied!" I cry out. "I was afraid this would be your reaction. How was I supposed to casually tell you I'm your biggest nemesis?"

Straightening, he says, "Well, at least you admit that."

"Jaxon, please. I wrote that stuff before I knew you."

"You still wrote it, Cara."

He has me there.

I figure that's the end of any discussion, but then he blows out a breath, and concedes, "Fine. You want to talk about this? Let's talk about it. Let's discuss how you wrote for me to 'put down the bong.' I don't even smoke weed, but do you know how many fucking people sent me fake bongs?"

"I didn't mean it literally," I say softly. "It was supposed to be tongue-in-cheek."

Jaxon scoffs, "Tongue-in-cheek, my ass. That was libel, and you know it. Do you realize the trouble I could get into if I really went out to play a game impaired? Hockey is my *job*, Cara. Do you fucking get that?"

"I know and I'm sorry," I whisper. "I am so, *so* sorry. I was wrong for writing that stuff. But I swear, Jaxon, I never meant to harm you. And I've learned a lot since then. I'd never do it again."

He softens, which hurts even more, especially when he whispers, "Here all this time I thought *you* made me stronger. But really you were the one stabbing me in the back. What a fool I've been. I don't even know who you are, Cara."

"Yes, you do," I say. "I'm still me."

"And who is that exactly? What else is behind your mask?"

"Nothing, I swear. There's no one else, no other secrets. Everything else I ever told you was the truth."

"The truth," he chuffs. "Do you even know what that word means?"

I start to reply, but then a horn honks. It must be his ride.

"Jaxon…" I reach for his arm, desperate because nothing has been resolved. And he's leaving, he's really leaving.

"Please don't go," I beg. "Not yet. We can work this out, I know it. We have too much to lose. I love you. And I'm sorry I hurt you, I swear that I am. But more than anything, I promise to never hurt you again."

Sloughing me off, he laughs bitterly.

"There's no need to make a promise like that, Cara. Because believe me when I tell you that you will never have *the chance* to hurt me again."

Turning away, he walks out of the house…and out of my life.

33

HOCKEY, THE ONLY THING LEFT

JAXON

I return to Las Vegas and immerse myself in the only thing that has any meaning left to me—hockey.

I do nothing but train for the upcoming season. It helps a little to blur the memories of my time on the island...and the person who shall remain unnamed.

I run, lift weights, and skate like crazy. I'm at the Desert Sports Complex, the arena where the Wolves play and practice, so often that ownership gives me a set of keys.

I try to encourage the guys that live in town to come practice with me, but it's a month before training camp starts and no one wants to burn themselves out.

Me, there's no chance of that happening. All my anger at the-one-who-shall-remain-unnamed fuels me, and I suspect that won't wane anytime soon.

"Cara," I murmur.

Aw, fuck. I said her name. Out loud too.

Whatever.

I still can't believe *she's* Mr. Hockeypants. If she'd only leveled with me from the beginning, maybe I could've accepted it.

Maybe.

"But she didn't even try," I hiss under my breath.

"Who didn't try?" a deep male voice responds.

Huh, what?

I just left the ice from a skate, and I'm in the locker room, alone, or so I thought.

I spin around and find one of my teammates, Dylan Culderway, standing in the doorway, arms crossed. Dylan is one of our top line defensemen, and a guy I really respect. So I'm cool with him hearing me voicing my meandering thoughts.

Still, I'm kind of surprised and end up saying the first thing that pops into my head.

"Hey, what are you doing here?"

Aw, shit, that didn't come out right. He has as much right to be here as I do.

But he takes it well.

Chuckling, he says, "Nice to see you too, Holland."

"Hell, you know I didn't mean it like that, Culderway."

"Yeah, yeah, I know."

I take a seat on the bench and rake my hands through my sweaty hair.

Dylan comes over and sits next to me, and again I try to explain my snippy comment.

"I just didn't expect to see you—or anyone, really—in here today."

"Hey, I told you no worries." He laughs. "I get it, you were surprised. Anyway, the reason why I stopped by is that I left a stick in here the other day." He gestures to a hockey stick leaning against the wall. "I like to practice with that one when I'm at home."

I nod in understanding.

Like a lot of us do, Dylan keeps a net in his basement to flick pucks into for practice. You can never get enough slapshot reps in. Not to mention, it's fucking fun.

And that gives me an idea…

"You've been practicing much lately?" I ask Dylan.

I'm hoping maybe I've finally found someone I can skate with here at the arena. I didn't bother him sooner because I know his wife, Chloe, is pregnant. I figured he was too busy with her for extra ice time. But I guess I was wrong.

"You mean here at the arena?" he clarifies.

I nod. "Yeah."

Shrugging, he says, "I've been coming in a little bit, yeah. Just to stay sharp, you know?"

I suggest then that since he's a defenseman and I'm offense, maybe we could run a few on-ice drills together.

"Some one-on-one work would be helpful to us both, eh?"

"Sure, that'd be great," he replies.

"Fantastic, awesome," I say, happy to finally have a practice partner.

Knowing that I won't be out on the ice all alone all the time makes me feel better than I have in a while. Plus, it's true that some one-on-one work will benefit us both.

Dylan and I then spend some time catching up on what we've been up to all summer. I try to keep the conversation focused on him by inquiring about Chloe.

"How's she feeling? She's due in the fall, right?" I say, putting on my super-interested face.

"She is," Dylan replies. "And she's feeling fantastic. Thanks for asking, Jaxon."

"Yeah, sure, sure. That's great, man."

"Yeah, it is. We're really excited for the baby."

I laugh, and Dylan says, "Hey, what's so funny?"

Shaking my head, I reply, "I just was thinking how it's crazy that I got to meet Chloe before anyone even knew you two were dating."

"Ah, yes, you sure did."

Dylan's a private guy, but I once caught him and Chloe at this very arena. They were, of all things, making out on the ice. Like literally sucking face on the blue line. It was in the early days of their relationship. They sure have come a long way since then. They're in love and working on building a family.

I sigh, thinking how that was something I was hoping for for me and Cara.

Too bad it will never happen now.

And that totally sucks because for as much as I hate Cara, I still fucking love her.

Damn it!

Dylan, watching me wincing—that's how much this shit still hurts—says, "Hey, is everything okay, man?"

I blow out a breath. "I guess so, more or less."

"That doesn't sound too convincing. Does this have anything to do with who you were talking about when I walked into the locker room?"

I admit, "Yeah, it kind of does."

"You want to talk about it?"

I almost say no, but if there's anyone to confide in, it's Dylan. He's the guy everyone goes to for advice. Well, either him or Nolan Solvenson, another player on our team. But since Dylan is here, and there's a shit ton of crazy weighing on my mind, I may as well open up to him. Lord knows it can't hurt.

"Actually, I could use some advice," I say.

"So, shoot."

I take a deep breath, exhale, and go on, "Did you know I was down at Noel's beach house for most of the summer?"

"I did hear something about that," he says.

I snort. "Of course you did. The hockey grapevine is rife with gossip."

"Not about everything," Dylan replies. "I only heard that you were down at the beach house, nothing more than that."

"Ah, well, my friend, there is so much more. The day I arrived, someone was already there."

He cocks a brow. "Let me guess, the person already there was a woman?"

"You got it." I say, smiling a rare smile. Yeah, it feels kind of good to tell my tale.

"Anyway," I go on, "her name is Cara. She's friends with Noel's sister."

"Ah, got it. So wires got crossed with Noel and Noelle and that's how you both ended up down there at the same time?"

"Pretty much," I reply. "But it wasn't bad. In fact, it was good…then it was really good. And then it was fucking fantastic." I sigh. "But it all fucking fell apart."

He looks lost after that synopsis, so I explain more coherently. I tell him all about Cara and the good times we had. I detail how we bickered like crazy, but then hooked up.

"I bet that was hot," he remarks.

"It was, but it was more than just lust, man. I may have sort of fallen for her."

"Sort of fallen for her?" Dylan raises a brow. "Did you fall for her or not, Jaxon?"

"Okay, okay, I did. But it doesn't matter, because we broke it off."

I leave out the reason.

Dylan seems to be contemplating something before he asks, "Does this Cara live far away?"

"No. That was the beauty of it. She lives here in Las Vegas."

Now my teammate looks utterly confused. "Wait. I'm not following. You said you two got along really well, right? You fell for each other *and* she lives in the same city that you live in. What the fuck's at issue here?"

I just can't bring myself to confess that she kept something important from me. Truthfully, I'm too embarrassed. I feel like I was duped.

So I simply state, "It just didn't work out."

Dylan doesn't press. He's not that kind of a guy. But since we made arrangements to start practicing together, I have a feeling this isn't the last conversation we'll have on the subject.

To be honest, I'm actually kind of hoping it's only the first.

Guess Cara Milne isn't out of my system quite yet.

Will she ever be?

34

THERE'S MY HEART, LYING ON THE FLOOR

CARA

After Jaxon leaves, I crumple to the floor, right in the middle of the entryway. I lie still and unmoving for hours, my cheek pressed to the cool, hard tiles.

I don't cry.

I'm in too much of a daze.

When I finally do stand up, I look down and I swear my heart is still on the floor where Jaxon left it.

"There's my heart, lying on the floor," I murmur as I back away, like the entry hall is a bloody crime scene.

In a way, it kind of is.

It's where my life was forever changed.

It's where my own crimes came to light.

The next few days, I exist in that same daze. I don't shower, I barely eat. I put in my earbuds to shut out the world. I play Miley Cyrus's "I Miss You So Much" loud and on repeat till my ears are ringing. I stay inside until I can't take it anymore.

When I finally do go outside to the back patio, I watch the lizards frolic and play. Even their cute antics can't make me smile, not anymore. They were my thing with Jaxon. And now their fun times are only a reminder of how we enjoyed watching them. And also of how Jaxon saved one the day we finally gave in to our lust and admitted our true feelings.

"Jaxon," I cry out, sending a lizard that had ventured close scurrying away. "See, I fuck up everything."

I have no one to blame but myself for this situation. Even though I hold out little hope of Jaxon ever forgiving me, I decide to place the blog on an indefinite hiatus. I guess I'm hoping he'll see that and know he means more to me than Mr. Hockeypants ever could.

I don't know if I'm secretly expecting him to call or text, but he does neither.

The only person I do hear from is Noelle.

Good thing too, as she reminds me that even though Jaxon and I are no more, I still have a life to live.

"Heartbroken or not, Cara," she says, "you can't stay down on the island forever."

"But you said I could stay as long as I like," I whine.

"Not to sulk. You need to come home and heal with people around you who care for you."

She has a point. Plus, there's something I need to do when I see her. I need to tell her that I'm Mr. Hockeypants. I left that part out of my sad Jaxon tale because I want to come clean in person.

That way if she wants to slap me, she totally can.

And I'll let her since I deserve it.

Sighing, I reply, "I know, Noelle. It's just that I hate the idea of coming back and running into him."

"This isn't a tiny town, silly," she reminds me, chuckling. "As long as you stay away from Wolves' games, you should be fine."

"Ah, that may be easier said than done," I murmur.

"What does that mean?" she asks, sounding perplexed.

"I'll explain once I get back."

A few days later, I'm back in good ole Las Vegas. I meet up with Noelle for dinner one evening after she's finished with work.

She looks amazing when she walks into the restaurant, all tall and elegant in her dark navy business suit, her platinum blonde hair done up in a twist.

I'm going to tell her tonight about Mr. Hockeypants, but not right off the bat.

"You look beautiful," I say when she grabs me up in a huge hug.

"You do too, Cara."

Stepping back, she holds our hands out in front of us and nods down to my white jean shorts and pumpkin orange tee. "Look at you, showing off your awesome tan."

I shrug and murmur a dead-sounding, "Thanks."

"Why do you sound so sad?" she asks. "You look stunning."

"It's just an illusion," I confess. "Inside, I'm kind of dying."

"Oh, sweetheart..." She pulls me in for another hug. "I want to know why this stupid Jaxon Holland dumped you. He must have taken too many hits to the head to let someone like you go."

I step back. "I'm afraid it's not that simple. I brought the break-up on myself."

"I doubt that," she says.

Ha, wait till she hears.

The hostess comes to seat us then, so our discussion is temporarily tabled. That's fine, since I have a feeling once I explain why Jaxon left, Noelle may very well have the same reaction.

Plagued with worry throughout dinner, I can barely eat. I pick at my salad as I listen to Noelle detail the latest news with her internship. But by the time the plates are cleared, she has me all up to speed.

"Enough about work," she says firmly. "I want the down-and-dirty Jaxon details. And let me tell you, if his reason for leaving you abandoned on that island is shitty, he and I are going to have a not-so-nice little talk."

"Trust me," I sigh. "He had a good reason for leaving, Noelle."

"Hmm, we'll see."

"No, he really did."

I put my head in my hands, and she blurts out, "Jesus, what the hell happened down there?"

Looking up, I cry, "Me, Noelle. I'm what happened. I fucked things up by lying to Jaxon about something *huge*. Actually, it's something you have a right to know too. And once I tell you, if you're done with me, I'll understand."

"God, Cara, what the hell is it?"

I may as well just dive right in...

"You know that Mr. Hockeypants blog?" I say softly.

"Sure. Everyone knows about it."

"Yeah, well, you know how Mr. Hockeypants's identity is this huge secret?"

"Um, yes."

"Well, not anymore." I gesture to myself. "Ta-da, you're looking at her."

"Wait, what? *You're* Mr. Hockeypants?"

It always comes as such a shock to everyone.

"In the flesh," I mutter.

"But…but…you don't even like hockey, Cara."

I wince. "Uh, that was just a ruse to throw everyone off."

She sits back. "Wow, it sure worked. You were very convincing."

"Are you mad?" I ask softly. "Do you hate me for keeping it a secret?"

To my relief, she says, "Oh, no, not at all."

I let out a huge breath. "Thank God."

"Cara," she says then, "I couldn't care less that you have a secret blogger identity. You're my friend no matter what."

Tears well in my eyes. "Are you sure?"

"Yes, of course I'm sure."

"Even if I did use some of the info you shared with me on the blog, some stuff about the players that Noel told you?"

She rolls her eyes. "I don't care about that. Those boys deserve to be called out when they engage in bad behavior."

"Oh, Noelle…" I swipe at the tears still welling, threatening to fall. "I can't believe you can forgive me so easily. You're making me cry."

Reaching across the table, she pats my hand. "Aw, don't cry, hon. It's how *I* feel, yes, but I have to be honest, I can see Jaxon's side on this too."

"I know, I know," I whisper. "I do too. Mr. Hockeypants has been anything but kind to that man."

"Yeah, he… Or rather, you really reamed him after that playoff loss."

I put my head in my hands. "Jesus, don't remind me."

When I look up, Noelle is scowling.

"What?" I ask.

She blows out a breath. "It's just that I don't think Jaxon should be so quick to throw true love away. What happened was bad, but not earth-shattering horrible. I don't know, maybe he'll come around. Maybe he just needs time to cool off."

"It's been three weeks since he flew back," I exclaim. "And he's not made a single move to get a hold of me."

"Have *you* tried to reach *him*?" she inquires.

"No. I've been too afraid."

"What are you afraid of, Cara?"

"I'm scared he won't respond," I admit. "Or that he will, and he'll tell me to never contact him again. I mean, he made it pretty clear on the island that he was done with me for good."

Noelle levels me with a no-nonsense stare. "Let me ask you one thing."

"Okay."

"Do you still love him?"

"Yes, of course I do."

"Then take out that phone of yours and text the man. Fight for him, Cara. If you do, and he's still done with you, then deal with it then. At least you'll know you tried."

She's right, so I take out my phone and text Jaxon that I'm back in town. I tell him that I still love him, no matter what.

I then add that I'm open to talk with him if he ever wants to.

With that, I hit Send.

And then the waiting begins…

35

SCHOOLED BY DYLAN CULDERWAY

JAXON

Just as I'm coming off the ice, after an impromptu evening practice with Dylan, my phone starts dinging, indicating that I have a text.

Huh, who could that be?

More and more guys are filtering back into town, readying for training camp, but I haven't been keeping up with anyone all that much. Dylan is the only teammate I have regular contact with, and that's only because we practice together.

As for the others, I've barely spoken with Noel. I hear he's back in town, but a girl he met in Sweden came back with him. I have a feeling there's a story there. I could call or text him for the deets, but if he's involved with this woman I'd hate to be reminded of how my relationship with Cara ended.

And that's what it would do.

My phone beeps again, so I grab it off the shelf from above my locker stall.

"Okay, okay," I bark to the insistent device. "You can shut the fuck up any time now."

You could say I'm a little cranky today. I thought that after a certain amount of time had passed, I'd feel better about breaking it off with Cara. But the opposite has occurred—every day that goes by without her in my life, I feel emptier. I miss our times on the island, but mostly I fucking miss her.

And that makes for one miserable motherfucker—me.

As I fumble to switch the phone over to vibrate, I catch sight of the screen and see who has texted—Cara.

My heart begins racing, and my palms start to sweat. She still has such an effect on me that I have to sit down.

Wow, this is like our first contact since the day I left her at the beach house. That day feels like a million years ago.

Yeah, it's been a million years of feeling miserable...or so it seems.

But I'm not miserable right now, knowing that Cara has texted.

I actually feel...happy?

But how could that be?

How could hearing from the one person who lied to me make me feel elated?

Because you still love her, dumbass.

"No, no. No, I don't."

I'm clearly in denial; even I can see that. But I just can't make myself read whatever it is she's texted. Frustrated, I toss the damn thing back onto the shelf without seeing a single word.

The phone makes an awful clatter just as Dylan's coming into the locker room. He always likes to stay out on the ice a little longer than I do. Too bad he didn't delay a few seconds more.

Now he's just witnessed my outburst.

"Whoa, someone's pissed about something." He lets out a low whistle. "I thought you got out all of your aggression on the ice, man. You went at it pretty hard."

"Yeah, I did," I grump.

"So why are you throwing shit around now?"

"I'm not," I protest. "That was just my phone."

"Did it do something to you?"

"Yeah, it wouldn't shut the fuck up."

I stare over at him pointedly, but Dylan isn't fazed one bit.

"Calm down, Holland," he says, chuckling. "You're not fooling anyone. Whoever was on your phone, they clearly have you all worked up. And I bet I know just who it is."

"Culderway, you're a fucking pain in my ass, you know that?"

I'm trying to sound angry, but it comes off as merely irritated. I want to be mad as hell at him, but I just can't. Dylan's intentions are always so fucking honorable. The dude really is a stand-up guy.

"I'm a pain in the ass all right," he volleys back. "That's why I'm going to ask you again why you won't give your girl another chance."

"She's not my girl," I snap.

"Save it, Jaxon. No man would be this upset over someone he didn't still care about."

He's right, but I insist, "It doesn't matter."

The conversation ends there, but I suspect it's only for the moment. I know Dylan. He can leave you alone forever. But once he decides he wants to know something, he's like a dog with a bone.

So yeah, he'll be back on me soon.

For now, though, we busy ourselves with taking off our pads and skates with our backs to one another. Still curious about Cara's text, I keep glancing up at the phone.

I'm torn between wanting to just go ahead and read what she wrote and wanting to throw the fucking device across the room. I could then watch it shatter into a million pieces. That'd be therapeutic, I bet.

Dylan's still quiet, so maybe I'm off the hook from any further questioning. But once he's down to a black tech shirt and hockey pants, he comes over and sits next to me on the bench.

"What?" I snap, casting him a side-long glance. "You need me to help pull your shirt over your head or something?"

"Ha-ha, Holland. You're real fucking funny today."

He shoots me a look that says *cut the shit*.

So I do.

"Okay, okay, what now?"

"Tell me why you broke up with Cara. You never gave me the reason, and I never pressed. But I'm pressing right the fuck now."

I blow out a breath, knowing I won't win this one. "You're worse than Dr. Phil, you know that?" I say.

"No, you dense fuck," Dylan retorts. "I'm just trying to be your friend. So start talking and who knows? Maybe I can help."

I close my eyes, and since he already knows the back story, I go ahead and blurt out the reason why we broke up, "She's fucking Mr. Hockeypants, okay? *That's* why I broke up with her."

Dylan totally misunderstands. "What? Cara's fucking that nasty blogger dude? How's something like that even happen? I thought you two were all alone down on that island. Had she met him beforehand? She must have, huh? Did he fly down to Florida to screw her?"

Oh, God.

For the first time in a long time, I break into peals of genuine laughter.

"No, no," I sputter between guffaws. "I didn't mean *that*. I meant she *is* Mr. Hockeypants."

He gets it then. "Oh? Ohhh… No fucking way."

My laughing stops then. "Yeah, I'm afraid so."

"Wow."

"You're speechless. Imagine how I felt."

He shakes his head slowly. "Dude, that is rough, no doubt. Mr. Hockeypants tore you a new one after our last playoff game."

"Tell me about it. My ass is still sore from that reaming."

"Well, if it's any consolation, I saw the other day that the Mr. Hockeypants blog is on an indefinite hiatus."

My brows shoot up. "Really? That's news to me. Not that I'd know. I never check."

Why would I go to that site? It'd only make me think of Cara. And I already can't get her out of my mind.

Clearing his throat, Dylan says, "Do you want my take on things? If not, just tell me to shut the hell up and I'll leave you alone."

I actually do want to hear what Dylan has to say. He's probably the most reasonable guy on our team. And he never gives shitty advice.

"Go ahead," I say. "I'd like to hear your opinion."

"Okay, well, first I need to ask you if you love her. Like really *love* her, man. Not just some case of lust or infatuation. That shit fades in time. And if that is the case, then I'd say cut your losses and move on. But if you love her for real—"

"I do, I do," I interrupt. "I keep trying to tell myself I don't, but I do. So just get to the point already."

Dylan chuckles. "All right, all right. What I'm trying to say is that if you love Cara you *should* give her another chance. Meet up with her, man. Give her an opportunity to fully explain. I bet that's why she's been texting you."

Balking, I reply, "Maybe. But I don't know, dude. If we start talking about that blog, I may lose my shit."

"No you won't."

"How can you be so sure, Culderway?"

"Because you're not a boy, Jaxon, you're a man. You made your point when you left the island, when you broke it off with her. Now it's time to decide if you want to fix things or not."

Damn, I think I just got schooled by Dylan Culderway.

36

PASSION REIGNITED AND SPUTTERED

CARA

Alone in my apartment, after dinner with Noelle, I'm plagued with second thoughts over having texted Jaxon.

It was a bad idea.

He's not texting you back.

He really is completely done.

Great, now I feel worse than ever.

Depressed, I curl up on the sofa. I'm still wearing the white shorts and orange tee I wore to dinner with Noelle. I should change into something comfier, like my pajamas, but I just don't have the energy.

At this point, I don't think I'll even make it to the bed.

I stretch out, ready to fall asleep on the sofa and put another day without Jaxon behind me. But just as I'm tugging on the soft chenille throw from the back cushion, to cover up with, my phone rings.

I pick it up and stare at it.

It's not a text coming in but an actual call.

And it's from Jaxon!

Eek!

My heart starts pounding like a little drummer has taken up residence in my chest. I'm afraid to answer, but I'm more afraid not to.

Hitting the green button, I croak out a shaky, "Hello?"

"Hey, it's me." Good, he sounds nervous too. "I, uh, just called to let you know I got the text you sent."

"You did? That's good."

I'm so smooth—not.

Jaxon clears his throat. "Yes, I did. It's good you made it back to town safely."

Annnd we enter completely awkward territory.

"Yes, the flights back were nice and noneventful," I reply.

He chuckles, which I take as a promising sign.

"Those are always the best kind."

"They are," I agree, nodding like crazy. I'm so *nervous*. "Better than eventful ones, that's for sure."

"Indeed."

This is so weird. It's like neither of us knows what to say. He's being nice, though, so there may be hope after all. We could at least be friends, right?

That possibility prompts me to ask, "Would you want to meet up sometime?"

Hesitating, he says slowly, "To do what?"

"Um, maybe we could talk?"

There's this really long silence, and I expect him to say no.

But to my surprise he utters a soft, "Okay. We could do that."

It's all I can do to contain my enthusiasm.

"Great, great, that's good." My heart is soaring and I can't settle it down. "When would be a good time for you?"

"What about now, Cara?"

Yikes. "What?"

There's a knock at my door. But what's weird is I hear it through the phone *and* in my living room.

Crap.

It's clear what the situation is, even as I whisper, "Y-you're here at my apartment?"

"Yes, I am—"

I don't give him a chance to say another word. Or maybe he is still talking, and I just can't hear because the phone is hanging half out of my hand as I jump up from the sofa.

Three seconds later, I'm swinging open the door.

And there's Jaxon.

I'm so glad I told him where I lived. I remember when it came up, during one of our long walks on the beach in the early days of getting to know one another.

Ah, good times.

I scan my gaze down the man I've missed like crazy.

Damn, he's still so freaking handsome.

He must've showered recently, as his sandy brown hair is damp and slicked back. His body looks really good too. He has on faded jeans that hug his muscular legs and a graphic tee with some band name on it that fits him perfectly.

His hotness is so all-consuming that I don't even take the time to see who the band is. Why would I care about his shirt when his eyes are meeting mine?

Wow, they look greener than ever.

Were they always this vivid and bright?

I think so.

It's just that they—and he—have been missing from my life.

I've missed you, I try to convey with my own eyes.

He smiles. And, Lord, that smile is utterly devastating. That's what gets me right then and there. It hits me like a bolt that touches my soul—Jaxon is actually *smiling* at me.

I almost start to cry. This is something I thought I'd never see again. Maybe there truly *is* hope for us.

I pray that that's true.

I smile back at him and for this good long while we just kind of stand there, smiling at each other and not saying a word.

I think his eyes are saying that he still cares, but that he's hurt.

I try to apologize with mine.

I think we may be on the right track, but when I reach for his hand, he takes a step back.

I act like I don't notice and clear my throat. "Uh, do you want to come in?"

I don't want him to turn around and leave. I don't think I can take him walking away from me a second time.

To my relief, though, Jaxon says, "Yeah, sure."

He comes in, and I close the door behind us.

"Would you like something to drink?"

I think about adding, *Water, coffee, a shot,* but I don't.

He replies, "Um, no, I'm good. I was practicing down at the arena with Dylan and drank a bunch of water before I left."

"Oh, okay. Then would you want to sit down?"

I gesture to the sofa, and he nods. "Okay."

Clearly we've reentered Awkward Town. That's reinforced when we sit at the same time and end up right next to each other, legs practically touching. Jaxon, though, hurriedly slides down to the other end of the sofa.

Ouch.

"All righty then," I can't help but snipe as my tension quickly turns to irritation.

He frowns. "What's that supposed to mean?"

I wave my hand dismissively, muttering, "Nothing."

"No, you made the comment, so it must mean something."

Hmm, Bickering Town is much more preferable than Awkward Town. It's where we lived for so long down on the island. It's a comfort zone of sorts, so I'm more than happy to take up residence there.

Digging in, I say, "Do you really want to know why I made that snippy remark?"

"No," Jaxon replies, sarcasm dripping like hot angry wax. "I'm just asking for my health."

"Okay fine, I'll tell you. Like I didn't notice how you scooted away from me...all the way down to the other end of the freaking sofa." I gesture sharply to where he's now smugly seated. "A bit of an extreme reaction, no?"

Those previously happy greens flash in irritation now. "Under the circumstances, Cara, I don't think so. A little space between us seems prudent."

"Like three weeks hasn't been enough?" I snap.

"Ha," he barks out. "Not nearly."

Ugh, he's so infuriating!

"You want space?" I practically yell. "I'll give you something better than space, buster."

I glare at him as I'm snatching two big pillows from a nearby chair. I then smack them down between us, creating a mini wall.

"How's a freaking barrier for you?" I narrow my eyes, challenging him. "Is that enough space now, Jaxon?"

Narrowing his eyes right the hell back, he snarks, "Not even close. Let's add one more."

Careful not to break our angry, dagger-throwing stare-off, he grabs a pillow from the floor and adds it to the pile.

It's a pretty big pile now, so big that I can barely see over the top.

In a way, he just won.

Bastard!

Sighing, I mutter, "Maybe I should just go sit over there." I motion to the big chair next to the sofa, the one from where I grabbed the pillows from.

Jaxon holds firm, snapping, "Maybe you should."

"Okay, that's enough," I growl. "Why are you even here?"

"Hey, need I remind you that *you* texted *me*, sweetheart."

I rise to my knees on the sofa cushions so I can see over the damn pillow barrier.

"That didn't mean you had to show up at my door!" I yell.

"Clearly, that was a mistake," he mumbles under his breath.

Ouch, again.

Hurt turns to ire and I stab a finger at him. "For your information, jackass, I texted you because I thought we could have a serious, adult discussion. I didn't reach out to play stupid fucking games."

He hops up onto his knees and points right the hell back. "You don't want to play stupid fucking games, eh?"

"Nope, I don't."

He laughs. "That's rich coming from the biggest game player

herself, Ms. fucking Hockeypants."

"That's *Mr.* Hockeypants to you, bud! You can at least get the name right."

"Oh, I know the name," he snorts. "Maybe I just don't care what the hell your slimy blog is called. As far as I'm concerned, shit is what it is!"

"Ugh, you, you…" I reach forward and with one sweeping motion, the pillows fly off the sofa.

Now there's nothing between us but hot, angry air.

"Go fuck yourself, Jaxon. I worked hard to make that blog a success."

With no barrier between us, he inches closer, jaw twitching.

"Like I haven't worked hard to get where I am? And here you come along, with your little Hockeypants blog, bashing the shit out of me. To the point where I had to leave town."

I wince, instantly feeling bad. But I'm still just so damn mad.

"I apologized for that!" I scream.

"There was more, Cara. You called me a dog, for fuck's sake!"

"I only wrote that because you were hitting up strip clubs night after night. If the shoe fits…" I mock.

"Hey, it wasn't *that* often. Do you even fact-check, honey?"

That catches me off-guard. "Wait, it wasn't?"

"No."

I get back to what's really important, at least to me. "Have you gone to any since you've been back in town?"

"Not that it's any of your business anymore, but no, I haven't felt like it."

"No?"

"Are you having trouble hearing, Cara? I said no."

We're both breathing hard, so hard, worked up from our screaming match. We're also practically leaning into each other now. Jaxon is so close that I can smell his yummy, soapy skin.

And it's divine.

This back and forth between us is driving me crazy.

I just want to…push him or something.

So I do—I place my hands on his chest and shove him as hard as I can.

He doesn't budge.

"Damn hockey players," I grind out, pushing harder.

Finally, I knock him off-balance and he falls backward onto the sofa. Or maybe he chose to give in, seeing as he takes me with him.

In any case, I end up on top of him and start scrambling to sit up. But that makes things worse because I somehow come out straddling him.

"Jeez, how'd that happen?" I murmur.

"I wonder," he deadpans when I make no move to get off of him.

He doesn't seem to mind. His hands are at my waist, steadying me, holding me in place. Not that I'm bothered. I'm rather enjoying the feel of Jaxon's hands on me. It's been so long.

I breathe out a jagged breath, and he slides his hands from my waist down to my shorts-clad ass.

Groaning, he palms my cheeks and starts slowly rocking me back and forth against the growing bulge in his jeans.

"You drive me nuts," he rasps. "Do you realize that?"

"Ditto, jackass," I moan.

"Fuck. Should we stop?"

"God, no," I gasp.

I guess that's all he needs to hear. He winds a hand into my hair and pulls me down to him.

"Kiss me like you mean it, sweetheart," he says.

Hell, yes. I kiss him like I mean it, and it's like coming home. He tastes so good and it feels so right to have his lips on mine, to feel his muscular body under me—to freaking dry hump him!

I go to town on that massive bulge in his jeans. Meanwhile, his hands are all over me—in my hair, ghosting over the sides of my breasts—like he can't get enough of me, either.

I break away, panting a breathy, "Wait, wait."

"What now?" he groans.

"Just... Does this mean we're back together?"

He looks at me blankly. "I don't know, Cara."

"Wait, what?"

It's like he just poured ice water over me. I sit up. But I'm still straddling him, so I slide back so that my damn crotch isn't all mashed up against his cock.

I need to think straight, damn it.

Shaking my head, I murmur, "If we're not working things out, then I don't think we should be doing this."

"Ugh." He scrubs his hands up and down his face. "You're killing me here, babe."

"I need to know something else too, Jaxon. Are you still mad at me over Mr. Hockeypants?"

"No...yes... Hell, I don't know."

"The blog is on hiatus," I say, hoping to prove that I take him having been hurt by my words seriously.

"I know, I heard."

Well, this is an interesting development.

"Who told you?" I ask.

"Dylan."

"So you were talking to him about us?"

"I was. But don't worry. He's a good guy who would never say a word—"

I wave my hand and interject, "I know, I know. It's okay. I don't mind. I talked with Noelle too."

He nods, and we're both quiet for a beat.

Finally, he breathes out a sad, "This is hard, eh?"

"It is," I agree, my heart skipping a beat.

He rubs his hand down his face again. "Shit, I was so mad about Mr. Hockeypants that I thought about suing his...*your* ass."

My eyes widen as I exclaim, "Jaxon!"

"Don't worry." He chuckles. "I'm not going to do that. Not now." His eyes tell me he'd never hurt me that badly.

I blow out a breath and offer, "Do you want me to just delete the whole thing? I'd do that for you if you really wanted me to."

I would. I'd pretty much do anything for this man. That's what love is all about, making sacrifices when needed.

He looks like he's thinking about it, but at last he says, "No. You said yourself that you worked hard to make it popular. I can't ask you to delete it. Besides, it's your livelihood, right?"

"Partly, but I really do have that trust fund I told you about. I *could* give up the blog if I had to. And"—I place my hand on his chest and peer down at him—"I would for you."

"Cara..." He places a hand over mine. "I told you that I'm not asking you to do that. But there is one thing I'd like to request."

"Anything," I say, "just name it."

"I'd like for you to consider changing your approach, like the way you blog. Mr. Hockeypants has the ability to cause real damage."

I sigh heavily. "I realize that now. And I'm already on it, Jaxon. I've been softening Mr. Hockeypants's image. Did you see the last post I put up before the hiatus?"

"I didn't," he admits.

"Well, it was about the Chidders trade."

"Oh, that dickhead," he barks. "Good riddance."

"See, that's my point. *You* don't even like him. But I was careful when I wrote the post not to say anything mean about the man."

Nodding pensively, he concedes, "That does sound like progress."

"It is, Jaxon. It's a real start."

"Yeah, I guess."

I sense he's drifting away, like the initial excitement of our reunion is wearing off and reality is crashing in. I know now that this isn't simply about the stupid blog. It's not even the words that I wrote. What we're down to now is that I lied to him. Not in the traditional sense, but in omitting an important fact. He had every right to know who he was getting involved with.

Sliding off him and back to my previous spot, I murmur, "We're not where we were, are we?"

He sighs and sits up. "No. It definitely feels different."

"Do you think it's because we're not on the island anymore? Or is it because of what happened?"

He shrugs and says, "Probably a little of both."

I then ask all that really matters. "Do you still love me, Jaxon?"

He reaches for me but stops himself.

"I do, Cara," he breathes out. "But I think I need more time."

"Okay," I murmur, looking away.

Smacking his hand down on the arm of the sofa, he snarls, "Jesus, I sound like such a pussy."

"No you don't." I venture a peek over at him. "You need more time,

I understand. I'm cool with that. Really, I'm just happy you don't totally hate me."

"Aw, sweetheart..." He reaches for me again and this time doesn't stop. "I could never, ever hate you."

I welcome his arm draped around me, even if it is just loosely. It reminds me of old times.

"Jaxon, can I ask you a question?" I say.

"Yes, of course."

"Do you think we'll ever get back to where we were?"

"I honestly don't know, Cara. Maybe in time?"

Time.

I better learn to love it, since it looks like I'm about to have a lot of it.

37

WELCOME TO THE WORLD OF LOVE

JAXON

Cara gives me what I ask for—time.

And I fill it with the same as before—24/7 hockey.

That works out well when training camp starts.

I'm all the way in too. I attend every practice. I arrive extra early and stay on the ice after all the other guys have left. Coach Townsend is so impressed with my newfound work ethic that he tells me he's going to make me an assistant captain this year.

"Wow, thanks," I say.

He replies, "You earned it."

I go at it even harder to prove he made the right decision. And then one day, after a particularly lengthy practice, he yells out over the boards, "Hey, Holland, get over here. I want to talk to you about something."

I skate over, noticing that I'm the only one still on the ice…as usual.

When I reach the boards, I notice a rogue puck wedged against the base. Fishing it out, I flick it across the ice and it goes right into the net.

Coach shakes his head and chuckles. "Nice shot."

"Thanks, Coach T."

He blows out a breath and gets back to why he had me skate over. "Jaxon, I called you over here because I've been waiting for a chance to talk to you alone."

Leaning on my stick, I say, "Why, what's up?"

"Nothing bad," he assures me. "I just want to tell you that I really appreciate the work ethic you've been displaying as of late. I feel good about giving you the assistant captain letter."

"Thanks. I'm happy to prove to you that you made the right decision. I am 100% devoted, Coach."

"Yeah, about that… It's kind of what I want to talk to you about."

I can't imagine where he's going with this, so I ask, "How so?"

He sighs heavily. "I just hope you know you can take time out for yourself and still be devoted to hockey."

"Sure." I nod. "I know that."

"Do you, though?"

"Um, yeah, I think so."

He glances down at his watch. "Look, it's after one. Do you want to grab some lunch with me? We can talk more candidly if we're sitting down, relaxed."

I'm torn. I am kind of hungry, and Coach is a cool enough dude, but with words like "candidly" and "relaxed" I sense he's hoping to dig around and find out what's really up with me.

Ugh, I don't want to talk personal shit with him.

Sharing my in-tatters love life with Dylan is more than enough.

But Coach is insistent, so I give in and go to lunch with him.

We choose the cafeteria in the Desert Sports Complex since it's convenient. Besides, by the time I'm showered and dressed, lunchtime is almost over. As it is, we make it to the cafeteria just in time before they stop serving food.

Coach orders the tuna melt, and I opt for a big-ass salad. I dig in the second we're seated, hoping to waylay any chance of discussing personal crap by stuffing my face. But since Coach's sandwich has to be made, he doesn't have food to occupy him.

That means he has nothing to do but chat.

And chat is what he does.

"So how was your summer, Jaxon?"

"It was good." I hurriedly stuff a cherry tomato in my mouth so I don't have to elaborate.

"I heard you were staying down at Noel's beach house."

"Yep, I was."

"Someone also mentioned in passing that you weren't down there alone."

Oh, *sure* it was in passing. I wonder who his source is. My money's on his daughter, Eliza. She's involved with one of my teammates, Benny Perry, and everyone knows he's a good guy but tends to blab *everything* he gets wind of.

I raise a brow and just flat-out ask, "You hear that from Eliza?"

Coach's tuna melt arrives just then and he messes with adjusting his sandwich for a good twenty seconds.

Any day now...

Finally, he looks up and says, "No, I heard it from Benny."

"I knew it," I exclaim. "That big lug's mouth is as big as he is."

That makes Coach laugh. "Aw hell, don't be mad at him, son. I think the whole team knows about you and…" He stops. "Wait, what's her name again? Oh, I know. Cara, right?"

Christ, it hurts to hear her name and know we're not together, even if it is me who asked for time.

"Great," I sigh. "The whole team knows, eh? That's just wonderful."

I groan. My private life is no longer private. But Coach is quick to inform me that no one knows the details. They're only aware that I was on the island with Noel's sister's friend. Everyone suspects we hooked up, of course, so they're kind of wondering why we're not together.

Upon hearing that, I growl, "It's none of their business."

"True, it's not. But I'm your coach and it becomes *my* business when I see you overworking yourself."

Uh-oh, we've reached the crux of the matter, the raison d'être for this meeting.

"I'm not overworking myself," I protest.

Though I really kind of am.

Coach puts down his sandwich. "Look, like I said, Jaxon, I love your dedication. But you're going to burn out before the season even begins. You're a key player, as you know. And we're going to need you at your best. We have a lot to prove after our dismal playoff performance last season."

I feel immediately guilty. "Tell me about it," I murmur.

Coach Townsend leans back, crossing his arms. "Can I offer you a bit of personal wisdom?"

I'm no longer hungry and push my salad aside. "Yeah, sure, shoot."

"I learned a lot watching my daughter and Benjamin Perry, especially in the beginning of their relationship. She kept something from him for a very long time, and it almost destroyed what they had built. But in the end, Benny realized what was important to him. Bottom line is that the past can never be changed. People make mistakes. It's bound to happen, and we can't control it. What we *can* control is how we deal with those mistakes. Do we dwell on the past? Do we make that person pay forever for the sin we feel they committed? Or do we forgive and move forward?"

Wow, Coach knows *waaay* more than he lets on.

But his advice is solid, so I feel okay saying, "I understand what you're talking about, and I don't disagree with you. It's just… What do we do if we forgive someone and they mess up again?"

Coach chuckles. "What? Do you think you're perfect, Holland? You think you'll never screw up or make a mistake? Or that you never have?"

"Good God, no," I chortle. "We all know that's not true."

I consider my own fuckups, like when I screwed up in the playoffs. Yes, mistakes happen. But still, I feel torn. We're talking about the heart here, where common sense flies out the window.

Raking my fingers through my unruly hair, I grind out, "Fuck, I just don't want to get blindsided again. That shit hurts like a motherfucker."

Chuckling, Coach says, "Jaxon, welcome to the world of love."

MS. HOCKEYPANTS

CARA

spend my time away from Jaxon doing what I should've done a long time ago—coming clean about Mr. Hockeypants.

That's right; I share with the world who I really am.

I reveal the woman behind the mask, exposing everything. I also explain that there'll be a new format for the blog and a kinder, gentler tone when it comes to real people. No more personal attacks.

Sure, I'll still call out bad plays, stupid moves, and the like, but no more mean-spirited crap.

I also change the name of the blog to reflect more who I am—Ms. Hockeypants. Yeah, I kind of got the idea when Jaxon called it that. But it makes sense. It fits me.

I expect to lose a bunch of followers, but a funny thing happens— the blog explodes with new subscribers. More people than ever seem to like the new Ms. Hockeypants, and traffic and views go through the roof.

My faith in humanity is restored.

Under my new moniker, I publish a post about the start of the preseason, titling it "It's the Best, Hockey-est Time of the Year."

I talk about new starts and how every team has a chance to go all the way. I review the rosters and discuss who I, Ms. Hockeypants, expect great things from. Jaxon Holland is one of my "Guys to Watch."

Once the post goes live, I hit my highest numbers ever.

Wow.

Sponsors and advertisers start coming to me and I receive all kinds of offers. I open the comments again, but with a warning to keep things civil. The love I receive for coming clean and making positive changes to the blog tell me I did the right thing.

This isn't for Jaxon anymore, or even for me.

This is for everyone.

I want to be a positive influencer in the world of hockey, not a Negative Nelly.

One night, when I'm basking in the glow of doing the right thing, I receive a call from Noelle.

She starts off the conversation like we spoke two minutes ago. "So guess what, biotch?"

"Hello to you too," I reply with a smile. She just slays me.

"Hey, there's no time for formalities. I have good news."

"Well, then." I laugh. "Do share."

"Yours truly has just won a two-night excursion to that posh new spa up near Mesquite."

"Ooh, lucky you," I reply. "I hear it's really nice."

"It is. Now I just have to figure out who to take."

"It's for two?" I ask.

"It is indeed, Cara. And you know what that means." She pauses for effect. "*You* are the one totally coming with me!"

"Really? No way." I'm all in and excited, but then I remember something. "Wait. Aren't those packages for couples only?"

"They are, yes."

"I feel bad, then. You should take a guy."

She snorts, "What guy? I don't have a boyfriend. Come on, Cara. There'll be free champagne and strawberries there. And I promise we'll have fun."

I laugh. "Let me guess, there'll be couples' massages and lots of candlelight too."

"Yep, and probably a big, heart-shaped bed we can share, though I promise not to steal all the covers."

"You're such a romantic," I tease.

"That's right, I am. So have I won you over yet with my smooth talk? Will you be my date?"

She's so silly.

"I don't know. When is this little getaway?"

"It's for Friday and Saturday night."

"Hey, Friday's my birthday," I exclaim.

"That's right. See, so you have to go now. I'm not about to leave you sitting home all alone, sulking over Jaxon on your damn birthday."

Ugh, I hate hearing his name.

Closing my eyes, I whisper, "We had plans for my birthday, Noelle, such big plans."

I think back to Jaxon's birthday and how wonderful that entire day was. I remember him promising to make my birthday just as special. Too bad I screwed up everything.

I sniffle, and Noelle says in a much more serious tone, "Cara, please come with me. I think it'll be good for you to stay busy. Let this be my birthday gift to you."

I think about it. She does have a point.

So I murmur a resigned, "Okay."

"Okay means you'll go?" she checks.

"Yes, I'll go."

We go over the details and disconnect.

Afterward, to my surprise, I'm actually smiling. Despite my initial hesitation, I feel excited about something. That hasn't happened in a while, so I guess I must be healing.

I muse out loud, "I just hope Noelle and I have fun." … "No, wait, I *know* we will."

No more wishes and hopes. I'm making things happen, damn it.

The spa excursion with Noelle is definitely the right decision. This is about moving forward, with or without Jaxon. What other choice do I have? I haven't heard from him, so who knows if he'll ever forgive me.

I have to accept the reality that he and I may be done for good.

That makes me sad, and I wish things were different, but I at least know now that if I have to move on without him, I can.

And I will.

Life will go on.

39

TOPPING NAKED BIRTHDAYS

JAXON

I put a lot of thought into what Coach Townsend had to say at lunch.

He's right—love is messy.

I guess since it's been so long since I was in any kind of relationship, I've forgotten the rules.

And the first rule is you have to forgive. People are going to fuck up. It's inevitable. Like Coach so wisely stated, you can't stop it. It's how you respond that's within your grasp.

I ask myself if I'm still mad at Cara for not telling me about Mr. Hockeypants. Like for real angry.

My answer is no, not anymore. It's in the past, where you can't change what's happened.

Do I wish Cara had told me that she was behind the blog before I inadvertently found out?

Sure I do.

But am I going to hold it against her forever?

No, I'm not. I love that woman, and nothing can change that fact.

So why am I still staying away from her?

Shit. Good question. And I don't really have an answer.

That tells me I don't need any more time. I'm ready to see if she'll have me back.

It's a Thursday morning and I'm on my way to the arena to slip in a short practice with Dylan. He and I decided to get in a little extra ice time before the Wolves' first preseason game, which is tonight.

I think about calling Cara right away.

When you realize you've made up your mind about something, especially in an affair of the heart, you sort of want to share the good news immediately.

But then I realize that this is too important for a rushed phone call. I'd much rather talk with her in person.

That way I can hold her, kiss her, love up on her...

When I walk into the locker room, I'm smiling like a fool. Dylan is already there and immediately takes note of my good mood. It's kind of hard not to when I'm all happy and upbeat.

Hell, I'm even whistling a little tune.

Damn, that's enough of that. Dude is going to think you've gone loco.

I quiet down immediately, but it's too late. Dylan has already heard enough of my out-of-tune melody to know something is up.

"Someone sure is happy this morning," he says, chuckling. "I know it is pretty awesome that you get to work out on the ice with me and all, but still, I'm truly touched, Holland."

"You're such an ass," I chortle. "And I hate to break it to you, but you, my friend, are not the reason for the whistling."

"No?" He covers his heart, pretending to be devastated. "I'm hurt, man."

Laughing, I take a seat next to him on the bench.

"You know what?" I say. "You've changed a lot from last season. You're actually a pretty funny guy, Culderway."

"Hey, I try to be these days. Chloe's always telling me that life's too short not to laugh."

"Amen, my brother."

He's lacing up his skates, but stops to look over at me. "You seem a little different yourself, Jaxon. You're not the same guy you were a year ago, or even last spring."

"What?" I laugh. "You mean I'm no longer an asshole?"

"Ah, hell, you were never that. You were just a guy trying to figure out who you were and what you wanted out of life."

I snort, "Is that a nice way of saying I was a player?"

"Maybe." He shrugs. "But I'll leave it at that."

"Fair enough, Dylan."

A beat passes, then he asks, "So the whistling and smiling when you walked in… Does it mean something good happened?"

I nod. "You could say that."

He raises a questioning brow. "Does it have anything to do with a certain someone named Cara?"

"Yep." I smile. "I've decided I want to be with her. I'm done being mad about all the Mr. Hockeypants crap. I understand now why she held off on telling me."

"Good for you," he says. "Oh, and by the way, it's not called that anymore."

"What are you talking about?"

"Her blog. It's now *Ms.* Hockeypants."

Well, this is news.

"You're shittin' me, right?" I say.

"I would never. Go check it out for yourself."

I do exactly that. I pull up the site on my phone and find out Dylan isn't lying. Cara's blog is indeed now called Ms. Hockeypants.

And there's more.

It appears she's made all the changes she told me about, and then some.

"Wow," I murmur as I scroll up and down, clicking links here and there. "She did everything she told me she was going to. And people really love it. Look at these great comments." I glance over at Dylan. "This is, like, *way* better than the blog was before."

He agrees, murmuring, "For sure."

I share with him then that I'm going to talk with Cara, but I want to do it in person.

"This is too important to discuss over the phone."

He laughs. "Hell, you just want to see her, man. Admit it."

"I do," I confess. "I miss her like fucking crazy. And I'm ready to end this stupid not-seeing-her shit. I just hope she still wants me."

Dylan replies, "Oh, I'm sure she will. Love doesn't just die like that. So, are you heading over to her place after we're done today?"

"I was going to, but I actually think I'll wait till tomorrow."

Dylan looks confused. "Why put it off?"

"Because, my man"—I pat him on the shoulder—"tomorrow just happens to be Cara's birthday. I figure we can celebrate that *and* the fact we're back together. It'll be perfect."

Dylan puts the brakes on my plans, though, when he frowns.

"Oh no, what's up?" I ask, worried.

"Uh, maybe nothing. But you might want to check with Noel first."

Jealousy flares. "What the fuck would he have to do with Cara on her birthday?"

Dylan holds up his hands. "Calm down, Holland. Not him, but his sister. He mentioned something about Noelle and Cara heading up to a spa in Mesquite for her birthday."

"What?"

He tells me again and I'm naturally disappointed.

But then I come up with an absolutely brilliant solution, a plan that's so good it may even top naked birthdays.

40

WOW, THE WOLVES LOOK FREAKING GREAT

CARA

I hunker down on the sofa to watch the first Wolves' preseason game, armed with a big bowl of popcorn and a beer.

I have my tablet handy as well, so I can take notes. I'll use them later to write up a Ms. Hockeypants post. All positive, of course, in keeping with the new blog tone and direction.

Though I don't know why I'm even worried. The Wolves come out flying on the ice, clearly pumped for this game against the Avalanche.

I'm not kidding. From the time the first puck is dropped, it is nonstop action. Brent Oliver, the captain, scores a goal in the first three minutes of play.

I jump up, spilling my popcorn. "Oops. I'll clean that up later."

Good thing I don't leave the room to grab a whisk broom and pan, because the Aves take a stupid penalty and the Wolves go on a power play.

I bite my lip. Shit, Jaxon's unit is up first.

"Go, baby, go," I murmur, brushing popcorn off my lap.

I swear my breath catches in my throat every time the puck touches Jaxon's stick. I'm sending him so many positive vibes it's not even funny.

It's not necessary, though. Jaxon and the whole team look more than ready for the regular season. This is only the first preseason matchup and they're already cycling the puck like old pros, dominating in all areas of play like they're well into the regular season.

Jaxon doesn't score on that power play, but he does on another one a short while later.

"Yes!"

More popcorn is spilled. But who cares? His goal is a beauty. And so are the others that come, even if they are from other players.

The Wolves win in the end with a final score of 5-1.

Yay!

Writing the blog post is actually fun.

I start by recapping the game, giving all the players lots of credit for their hard work and success. Of course, I can't help but lay it on thick for Jaxon, remarking on how he obviously worked *extremely* hard in the offseason.

I giggle to myself, thinking how I contributed some to those workouts. I mean, surely all the sex we had all over the beach house played a small part in keeping his cardiovascular endurance up.

I keep that tidbit to myself, though.

But it sure makes me smile.

Damn, I miss that man.

After I publish the blog post, I head to the bedroom to start packing for the spa trip. I'm meeting up with Noelle tomorrow, but not at check-in. We were supposed to drive up together, but she texted me earlier to tell me she'll be running late. She gave no explanation as to why.

Weird.

Ah, well. I can only assume it has something to do with her classes. Grad school started back up for her recently.

Anyway, she insisted someone has to be at the spa at three sharp in order to officially check us in. Otherwise, the staff could think we bailed and give away our free room.

I don't know. I suspect they'd hold our reservation till midnight, but whatever.

After I toss what I think I might need into an overnight bag, I get ready for bed.

A few minutes later, I'm resting my head on the pillow. But then I notice it's after midnight.

"Happy Birthday," I whisper to myself. "Make a wish."

I sigh. Too bad it's not Jaxon whispering those words to me. During the summer, I thought it would be. Until it all fell apart.

So here I am all alone.

Choking back a sob at that realization, I finally get around to making a wish. It's an easy one—I wish Jaxon and I could work things out and get back together.

If only birthday wishes really did come true.

THE SWITCH

JAXON

After the mini practice with Dylan, I get to work on my covert plan for Cara's birthday.

First, I contact Noel.

"Hey, uh, I hate to bother you," I begin. "But I have kind of a weird request and it really can't wait."

Always amiable, Noel replies, "Hey, that's cool. You're not bothering me, anyway. Whatever you need, Jaxon, just name it. I'll do what I can."

Wow, that was easy. He's such a cool dude.

"Great," I exclaim. "I need your sister's number."

"Uh…"

Okay, maybe not so easy after all. Noel's such a laid-back guy, but not so much when it comes to his twin.

Sure enough, bristling, he says, "Look, Holland, I know you're hurting right now. But I'm not about to facilitate you hooking up with Noelle."

Rolling my eyes, I try not to laugh. "Don't worry. I don't want to hook up with your sister. I just need her number so I can ask her something, okay?"

Still sounding suspicious, he says, "What do you want to ask her?"

"I have a question about that spa trip she's going on with Cara."

"Ah, I see. How do you know about that trip, anyway, Holland?"

Oh, jeez. "Dylan told me."

"Aha."

I figure now's as good a time as any to just lay it on the line. I don't have time to go around in circles. Plus, Noel is going to continue to think I'm after his sister if I don't come clean.

Blowing out a breath, I say, "Let me just ask *you* something, okay? I think it'll clear things up."

"Sure, Jaxon, go ahead."

"Do you think your sister would be up for swapping places with me on that spa trip? I'd love to be there and surprise Cara."

He snickers, clearly relieved.

"Hell, yeah," he says. "I'm pretty sure Noelle will be all over that. She's a huge romantic."

Knowing his sister is safe from evil-me, he finally gives me Noelle's number, and I call her as soon as he and I disconnect.

She seems a little weirded out that I'm contacting her, until I explain the situation.

"Oh my God, I am so sorry I was snippy at first," she says.

"Not a worry," I reply.

You sure can tell she and Noel are twins.

But he was right about her.

Excited, she exclaims, "And, Jaxon, I love your idea. Cara's absolutely going to die when she sees you at the spa instead of me."

I breathe a sigh of relief. "You don't think she'll punch me in the junk and kick me to the curb?"

"No way! I think she likes your junk way too much."

I preen a little. "She does, eh?"

"Hey, don't be getting all cocky on me. I didn't say she wouldn't kick you to the curb. I just said your manhood will likely remain intact."

"Thanks," I deadpan. "That's like good news, bad news."

"Eh, it is what it is," Noelle sighs. "You created this situation by needing extra time."

"I know, I did," I sigh. "And it went a little longer than I expected it to. But I'm all in now. I've fully forgiven Cara."

"Well, that's good, Jaxon. But you still better do right by her. If I hear one word about you being a dick, *I* will do what Cara never would. I'll kick you in the junk."

"Ouch," I murmur, covering said junk even though Noelle isn't here.

"Just be good to her, Jaxon."

"Okay, okay, I will. I plan to be, all right?"

"Hmm…" she murmurs, still not sounding completely convinced.

Jesus, Noel's sister is tough. Of course I'll be nothing but good to Cara. I freaking love her.

"So," I breathe out, "you sure you're okay with me going to the spa in your place? I'll pay for you to go another time if you want."

"That's nice of you, Jaxon. But don't worry about it. I'm definitely fine with you going in my place. Just make Cara happy."

"That's the plan," I assure her. And then I check, "You won't let anything slip about this, right?"

"Of course not," she laughs. "My lips are sealed."

We plot out the details then, so neither of us fucks this up. We spitball a ton of options, but decide on something that'll ensure that Cara drives up to the spa alone. If she bails, I'm toast.

"I can't tell her I'm not coming," Noelle says. "She definitely won't go then."

"True. And that would totally suck."

"It would, Jaxon. So look, I think I should text her that I'm going to be running a little late tomorrow. Don't worry, I'll be vague. But I'll stress the need for her to arrive by three to check us in."

"What time is the check-in for real?" I ask.

"It's at two."

"Perfect! I'll arrive early and I'll check us in ahead of time. That'll give me an opportunity to set up things in the room. I'll also explain to the front desk that it's a birthday surprise for my girlfriend, and for them not to mention that I'm already there when Cara 'checks in' later."

"Does that mean she's your girlfriend again, Jaxon?"

"Well, that's up to her," I reply honestly. "I told you that I'm all in. So the ball's in her court now. But I think if all goes well this weekend, she will be my girlfriend again."

42

SURPRISE!

CARA

I arrive at the spa at three on the nose. It's a really gorgeous property with gardens and fountains everywhere. When I check in at the front desk, the employees are all giggles and smiles. It's like they're in on some secret that everyone knows about but me.

But that can't be right.

Okaaay, now you're imagining things, Cara.

Great, for my twenty-third birthday, I'm losing my mind.

Sighing, I proceed to the elevator to make my way up to our assigned room, #247.

Once I reach the second floor and step out of the elevator and into the hall, I send Noelle a quick text to let her know I'm at the spa.

Strangely, she doesn't reply back.

That's odd, as I haven't heard from her all day. I guess she's tied up with whatever prevented her from coming up on time in the first place. Still, you'd think she'd be on the road by now. At this rate, I'll be hanging in the room alone for the next couple of hours.

At the door to the room, I fumble with the key card. The straps of my overnight bag and my purse keep falling down my shoulder. *Damn.* It takes six tries to finally get my butt, and my bag and purse, in the room.

"Ugh, I should've just stayed home," I lament as I struggle when the door keeps falling back on me.

My mood is quickly lightened, though, once I'm inside the spacious room.

Wow, the whole place smells wonderful. And no wonder. There are pretty bouquets of colorful flowers in vases all around. Like I mean they're everywhere—on the dresser, on the nightstand, on the counter in the bathroom. There are even pink and red rose petals scattered across the big heart-shaped bed. A few lit candles dot the room as well, adding to the ambience.

I sigh. This room is ideal for romance. Too bad it'll just be me and Noelle. This space, clearly set up for love, will sadly be wasted.

Ah, what can you do?

When I toss my bag and purse onto the bed, I notice there's an outdoor balcony just off to the right. I can't see the view, however, as the drapes are drawn.

Again with the romantic touch.

Well, I'm not here for that.

Huffing, I stomp over to the balcony door and gingerly yank the string to open the drapes all the way.

"What the hell!" I cry out. "There's a naked man out on my balcony!"

But, hmm, he's not bad looking. At least, his back view is good.

Lucky for him this part of the resort is located in the back of the property, where there's nothing but desert and mountains. Not that I'm checking out those. No, that's purely background. I'm too busy zoomed in on this dude's broad shoulders, muscular legs, and the firmest, most perfect ass.

I realize then that I'm not freaked out because I know that ass.

But, wait, what's *he* doing here?

Mildly pleased but unsure of what this could mean, I slide open the door and murmur a tentative, "Jaxon?"

He turns around, and that face. Damn, I've missed him so much.

"Surprise!" he says with a big ole grin.

I'm speechless. This is the best freaking surprise ever, especially on my birthday. Too bad I'm too stunned to share that with him.

Naturally, my silence has Jaxon worried that we're about to reenact our first meeting. You know the one, where I caught him with his hand on a certain part of his body and I promptly hurled a planter at him.

Covering his head—and not the one at the top of his body, mind you—he says worriedly, "You don't have any of those glass flower vases hidden behind your back, do you?"

I can't help but laugh. "No, I swear that I don't."

I hold my hands out in front of me to prove I'm not armed with dangerous projectiles.

He breathes a sigh of relief and drops his hands away from his junk.

Wowza!

I forgot that, even when not hard, Jaxon possesses a very impressive cock. My lady bits didn't forget, though. They twinge at the memory of what he can do with that thing.

"Oh, Jaxon…" Confusion and wanton lust war within me. "What are you doing here?"

He winks. "Let's just say Noelle and I worked out a plan that involved us switching places for this trip."

Well, this is news. "You mean she's not coming?"

"No." He raises a questioning brow. "Are you disappointed?"

I shake my head. "Of course not, but what does this mean exactly?"

"It means that I want you back in my life. If you'll have me, that is. I miss you, Cara, and I love you. Not to mention that I want you back in my bed."

Another twinge, and then I nod to where he's semi-hard. "Um, I can see that last part is true."

"It's all true, babe."

I'm tentatively hopeful as I ask, "Really, Jaxon?"

"Yes."

I realize then that he's still out on the balcony, naked and professing his love. It's so funny that I have to laugh.

That, of course, makes him laugh too.

God, I've missed that, us laughing together.

That's when my heart skips a beat.

Could we really be working things out?

Could my birthday wish be coming true?

He's saying all the right things, but is he still angry over Mr. Hockeypants? I have to know.

So I ask, "You're not mad at me anymore for not coming clean about the blog and knowing all about hockey from the start?"

"No," he says, his voice becoming raw and rough.

My breathing quickens. I want him, and it's clear that he wants me. Play time is over, shit's about to get serious.

I back up into the room and he follows, sliding the door closed behind him.

I keep moving backward. But I don't go too far. I stop a few feet from the bed, and that's when I notice it's so, so quiet. There's no more noise from the outdoors, like how it was with the door open. However slight those sounds may have been—birds chirping, the wind kicking up, traffic in the distance—they buffered us.

Now it's just me and Jaxon, about to bare our souls.

"Do you want me back, Cara?" Jaxon asks. "Will you *take* me back?"

I'm not making the same mistake as last time, going straight to the physical and then discovering he's not ready for more than just that.

Raising a brow, I query, "I thought you needed time?"

"I had time. And fuck needing any more of it. I finally realized that time is too precious to waste. The only 'time' I need now is more time spent with you."

"Okay, then." I nod, taking that all in.

He then asks again, "Do you still want me? Like, in your life?"

Is he kidding?

"God, yes," I breathe out. "I want you in *every* way, Jaxon. In my life, inside *me*—"

"Then fuck this shit."

He descends on me then, kissing me with unleashed urgency as he slowly walks us back to the bed. His hands are busy, as are mine. Between the two of us, the shorts and flowy blouse I was wearing end up on the floor. Panties and bra are next. And soon I'm naked and bare just like Jaxon.

Softly, I murmur, "I love you so much. And I've missed you like crazy too."

He groans as he lowers his warm mouth to my breast, where he flicks my nipple with his tongue. He sucks and nibbles, then moves to the other breast to do the same thing. It's like he's relearning the taste of me. And I gasp in pleasure as he rediscovers.

But I want so much more.

"Touch me while you do that," I demand.

Yep, this is me, asking for what I want.

And Jaxon gives it to me.

His hand skims down my abdomen where he plies my clit in tandem with the movements of his tongue on my breast.

I soon feel a release building. It's been so long. *Too* long.

But before I reach the apex, he changes things up.

"Damn, I love your spontaneity," I murmur, "even if it does frustrate the hell out of me. I was so close, Jaxon."

"Don't worry, sweetheart," he replies with a twinkle in his eyes as he peers up at me from where he's now kissing his way lower and lower. "You're going to really love this next part."

"Oh, no," I rasp, teasing. "What ever are you doing?"

"Oh, yes," he volleys back. "You're about to find out."

His mouth then closes over where I ache for him the most, and I cry out, "That feels so amazing, Jaxon."

"I told you it would," he murmurs, taking a breath.

And then he gets back to making things even more amazing. A few skillful moves of his tongue, and I fall over the edge.

But before I can catch my breath, I'm tossed onto the bed. The hunger in Jaxon's eyes as he crawls up over me is unmistakable. He's about to devour me.

And I can't wait.

"Don't go easy on me, Jaxon," I purr.

"I wasn't planning on it," he growls.

Fuck, he's so delirious for me I can feel it in the air. It's like electricity. I play into it, amping him up even more as I lie back and spread my legs. The soft, silky petals stick to my back and my ass, making everything feel decadent.

Jaxon hovers over me, and I place my hands on his ass, urging him to lower his body down to mine. I just want him so badly.

"Take me, Jaxon," I plead. "Make me yours again."

"Cara…"

Lowering himself, our skin touching in all the right places, he thrusts into me roughly.

"Yes!"

It's raw at first, on both our parts. He thrusts and pistons into me as hard as he can. And I love it. I need this. I need *him*. I lift up so I can take more of him since I can't get enough of this man.

And in that frenzy, our bodies work out what we haven't yet said.

But eventually we both give in…to each other. And from that point on, it's all love, love, and more love.

We're finally back to where we were, but it's better because this is a new starting point. We've grown, having gone through a relationship hardship…and coming out stronger.

The electricity in the air finally settles to a warm current, and I whisper, "This is perfect."

"It is," he agrees, slowing his pace even more.

We rock together slowly, with him just rolling his hips gently, loving me easily.

The fight is gone.

We've made peace.

Pressing his cheek to mine, he whispers in my ear, "Happy Birthday, my love."

I reach up to touch his lightly stubbled cheek. "Thank you. And by the way, you did it, Jaxon."

He leans back and looks at me, confused. "I did what, babe?"

"You made this my best birthday ever. Remember when you promised that you would?"

"Of course I remember. But…" Rolling onto his back, taking me with him without breaking our connection, he says, "…I'm not anywhere near done yet."

"Ooh, you're not?"

"Not even close. And I just realized something too."

"What's that?"

"Naked birthdays are still the best."

I can't disagree. "They sure are," I proclaim.

I circle my hips, and he growls, "Enough talking. Love me, woman."

"I already do, Jaxon."

"So show me how much."

Ah, that I can absolutely do.

43

OUR OWN LITTLE WORLD

JAXON

Even though the spa retreat package Noelle won includes couples' massages and several therapeutic treatments, Cara and I scrap them all.

Who needs those when you're living on love?

Not us. We have no reason, or desire, to leave the room. Though we do accept the complimentary strawberries and champagne the staff sends up to us, mainly because we're famished.

I must admit they're not solely for sustenance, though. Cara and I find some interesting things to do with both items.

Ah, kinky times are good times.

But it's not all kink and sex. Cara and I have created our own little world. We're back on the island in our minds. Hell, there's even sand outside, so close enough.

Sadly, though, there's no beach.

That night I'm thinking all these things as I'm out on the balcony, peering off into the darkened desert. That's when Cara comes up from behind me.

"Hey, sweetheart," I throw out over my shoulder, having heard her soft footsteps.

She wraps her arms around me and leans her head against my back. "Hey, Jaxon," she murmurs.

It feels like she has on her short, filmy robe, as her nipples are taut against my bare back. Good thing I have on boxer briefs, or I'd turn around right now and have her again right here out on the balcony.

"What are you doing out here, Jaxon?" she asks, distracting me from my sexy meanderings. "I thought you said you were coming right back in."

"I am." Turning around, I place my hands on her hips. "I was just out here thinking about things and I guess I got lost in that."

Tilting her head, she queries, "What were you thinking about?"

I smile down at her. "Mostly just about how much I miss living with you at the beach house."

She sighs. "I know. I miss it too. We had some great times there, yeah?"

"We sure did. They were the best."

"I wish we could go back, Jaxon, even for just a few days."

"I do too," I say.

I think about it for a minute and add, "Hey, you know what? I think maybe we *can* go back."

"Yeah," she says, sighing. "I know. But not till next summer. And that's such a long time away."

"No, no, I think we can go before then," I say excitedly.

She peers up at me with those pretty hazel eyes that I've missed so much and says, "I don't see how, Jaxon. You have games way into the spring, and even longer if you guys make it to the playoffs."

"Whoa, hold up!" I exclaim. "You mean *when* we make it to the playoffs."

She giggles. "Yes, definitely, that's what I meant."

I finally get to the point and share with her what I'm thinking.

"All that's true, but you're forgetting one thing. The Wolves have a longer than usual Christmas break this year. Sooo, if we really want to, we can head down to the beach house then. That is, if it's okay with Noel, of course."

Her eyes brighten. "Oh my God, I love that idea."

"So you'd want to do that?"

She nods. "Definitely."

What I don't tell Cara is that if all goes the way I think it will over the next few months, we're going to have more than just time off to celebrate down at the beach house.

I'm going to ask her to marry me.

THE HOCKEY LIFE

CARA

O nce we're back in Las Vegas, the weeks fly by.

Now that we're officially back together, Jaxon and I try to spend as much time as possible together. Two preseason away games put a pause on our constant hanging around each other. But with home games and practices the rest of the way out, we're afforded plenty of time to share.

And that's what we do.

We go on dates and sometimes just chill at my place or his. Jaxon's house is not as large as some of the other hockey players' places, but it's nicely decorated and surprisingly cozy.

Who would've thought?

Not me. I expected it to be your typical bachelor pad. I like that Jaxon is always full of surprises. It's been that way since the start when

I caught him in that very compromising position.

I have to snicker now, thinking of how he nearly recreated that same day when we were at the spa resort. After all, he was outside. He just didn't have his hand on his cock.

But I sure did—later that afternoon, that night, and the next morning.

"What are you thinking about, babe?"

Jaxon has just sauntered into the master bedroom at his house and is staring at me sitting cross-legged on his big bed.

"Your dick," I reply truthfully.

He gives me a *not-now* look. "Babe."

He shakes his head, and I feign innocence. "What?"

"You're bad."

I am, seeing as it's time for him to leave for the first game of the regular season. Oh, well, maybe this will wind him up and he'll score—on the ice, and then later back here at home.

Pointing to me, he says, "You're lucky I have to leave in, like, three minutes. Otherwise I'd have you flipped over on that bed so fast..."

I raise a brow. "Hey, I'm up for a quickie."

I'm insatiable when it comes to Jaxon.

Chuckling, he says, "Problem is, sweetheart, it's never quick with us."

Hmm, he does have a point. We always end up lost in worshipping each other's bodies. And then time slips away.

"Later?" I waggle my eyebrows.

"Do you even need to ask?" he chortles. "With us, I think that's pretty much a given."

I smile. "True."

I can hardly wait for later, but I must. His game comes first. Good thing I'm going with Noelle. She's my ride to the arena, but we plan to sit together as well.

Jaxon is eyeing me curiously, so I ask, "What now?"

"It's just..." He nods to my attire. "Are you wearing *that* to the game?"

I peer down at the ragged super short shorts and thin tee I have on, and shaking his head, he adds, "You're gonna be hella cold in the arena."

Quickly, I inform him, "Don't worry, I'm changing. I have time, though. You may have to leave in a couple of minutes, but Noelle won't be here for another hour."

"So what are you wearing?" Jaxon wants to know.

"I was thinking skinny jeans and a Wolves' jersey."

He stops and cocks a brow. "A Wolves' jersey, eh? What number's on it?"

Ah, this is where he's been going with all the questioning. But he needn't worry.

I answer proudly, "Why I'm wearing number twenty-three, of course."

That's Jaxon's number, and he happily replies, "Aw, that's my girl."

I am. I'm his girl in every way.

That's why, a short while later, I'm whooping it up and high-fiving Noelle—*and* high-fiving four random strangers seated around us— when Jaxon scores a beautiful goal during the first period.

Noel gets the assist on it, so Noelle's happy too.

The Wolves are playing the Kings tonight and kicking their asses. And the whooping doesn't end after the first. Brent Oliver, in the opening minutes of the second period, scores too. Next, there's a reach-around shot from behind the net that puts Nolan Solvenson on the board.

Everyone's really happy about that one, as Nolan's obviously come back strong from his wrist injury last spring.

Best part of all this scoring is that we're only halfway through the second period. If this is a preview of things to come, the Wolves are sure contenders to go all the way.

After the game, I have Noelle drop me off in the players' parking area. There's no need for her to drive me home when I can just head back with Jaxon. After all, we have plans to continue what we started earlier in his bedroom, right?

I texted Jaxon before we left the complex, letting him know I'll be meeting up with him. So he's not the least bit surprised when he sees me walking toward him in the parking lot.

But he sure is happy.

Grabbing me up in his arms as soon as I reach him, he spins me around in a big circle and says, "What a game, eh?"

After kissing him lightly on the lips, I reply, "Yes, it was fantastic. You guys looked incredible."

"Thanks, babe. That means a lot."

He sets me down so he can adjust the strap of the bag slung over his shoulder.

"Did you see my goal?" he asks when we start over to his SUV.

"Pfft, are you kidding me? I saw it and I went nuts. I think the people around me thought I'd lost my mind."

"Oh, speaking of your seat, that reminds me. I was able to reserve you a spot in the players' wives and girlfriends section. Family sits there too, so Noel reserved a seat for his sister as well. I think they're side by side, so you guys should be able to sit together all the time."

"That's great, Jaxon." I take his hand. "Thank you. That was really sweet of you."

Smiling down at me, he replies, "For you, babe, anything."

"Hmm, well if that's true, then you won't mind if I write up a quick blog post before we go to bed?"

I raise a questioning brow, and he says, "Hmm, as long as it doesn't take *too* long"—he squeezes my hand—"then sure, I can wait."

Now that the blog is a whole different incarnation of its former self—and even more popular, I might add—Jaxon is fully supportive.

I think about how we got to where we are. We're in a really good place, that's for sure. Though it's not been reached easily, it's been worth every good and bad moment.

From me and Jaxon working through our initial constant bickering, and then reaching a shaky truce, to finally falling in love.

We fell in love, but then we fell apart, thanks to Mr. Hockeypants.

But that's all behind us now.

I'm Ms. Hockeypants these days. And Jaxon and I are together and so very much in love.

Suddenly a big, bright star streaks across the inky night sky.

"Cara, look," Jaxon exclaims, pointing up into the darkness. "It's a shooting star."

"That is so cool," I gasp in awe, my face tilted upward.

We stop and watch the trajectory of the star, and then Jaxon nudges me. "Hey, you have to make a wish now. But you can't tell anyone what it is."

I nod. "Okay, but only if you make one too."

He agrees, and we turn to each other, hands joined.

My wish is easy—I wish for us to be together forever. I even want to someday be his wife.

When I look into his eyes, I'm pretty sure he's thinking something similar. He wants us to be together forever, and he wants to marry me too.

Somehow, I just know that.

Call it intuition or call it crazy, I don't care. I just know all of our wishes will come true.

After all, it's now written in the stars.

EPILOGUE

FULL CIRCLE

JAXON

I make the necessary arrangements with Noel to stay at his beach house over the holiday break. He informs me that the housekeeper will stock whatever food and necessities we'll need, just like she did in the summer. He also lets me know that he hired a new groundskeeper. He didn't like the little lizards being trapped any more than Cara or I did, and he just couldn't trust that guy.

Guess we're all animal lovers, even when it comes to reptiles.

Once everything is set with the beach house, the secret part of the plan I came up with long ago is in play—I'm going to ask Cara to marry me.

No one knows, though, just me.

And I can't wait.

I'm counting down the days because I want her in my life forever. I knew that from the day of our reunion, but I became more certain the night she and I saw the shooting star. There was just something in her eyes, like we were wishing the same thing.

I wished upon that star for us to be together forever, and I wished for her to become my wife.

And I've been waiting since that night, biding my time, in anticipation of our return to the island.

Everything has to be perfect for this proposal. It needs to fit *us*.

That makes me think back to the first time we met, when she caught me, uh, engaging in self-satisfaction and threw a heavy planter at me.

I chuckle at the memory. It's funny now, though it wasn't then.

Hell, maybe it was a little. No one was really hurt, right?

I decide then to arrange my proposal around that first encounter. It's a day that's a part of our history, just like the island and the beach house are. Maybe someday I'll freaking buy the place from Noel. It means that much to me, and I know it does to Cara as well.

But for now, I'm focusing on the proposal.

I think I know how to make it perfect.

The day after Christmas, Cara and I fly down to the island on a private jet I charter. Having spent the holiday with my family and hers—spread out over Christmas Eve and Christmas Day—we're pretty much exhausted.

When we're about halfway to our destination, Cara yawns and says, "Oh my goodness, Jaxon. This Christmas has been tiring. I'm so sleepy."

Leaning over the arm of her seat, the one by the window, I deposit a quick peck on her cheek.

Yeah, just a peck for now. I'm saving all my really good kisses for when we're at the beach house.

"Why don't you rest for a while," I murmur in her ear.

"Mmm"—she slouches down—"I think I will."

Cara's out almost instantly, which is good since I plan to wear her out all over again once we're on the island. Speaking of which, I should catch a few z's myself.

I nod off quickly, and the next thing I know we've landed.

That evening, I fire up the grill out on the back patio and make us a delicious steak and grilled veggies dinner.

"Hmm, so you made the same thing we had for our first meal together," Cara remarks just as we're finishing up.

I wink over at her. "I did. It's all part of my grand scheme for this trip, babe."

She raises a brow, stilling the wineglass she was lifting to her mouth. "Grand scheme, huh? Does that mean we're reenacting our first day on the island?"

I shrug, giving away nothing.

Glancing around the patio with a wicked grin, she says, "Well, it seems we must be. But we're a little out of order on events, yeah? As I recall, the steaks were later in the day. Out on this patio here, I caught you naked and uh—"

I hurry to interject, "Yeah, we're deviating from that part somewhat."

Curiosity fills her gaze. "Do tell me, how so? Because I have to say, Jaxon, I like you naked."

This woman.

I laugh and lean across the wrought iron table as I assure her in a whisper, "I like you naked too. So that means when I take off my clothes tonight, you bet your sweet ass yours are coming off right along with mine."

"Ooh, Jaxon."

After taking a quick sip, she sets the wineglass on the table with a *clink.* "Why wait?"

"That's my girl."

She is my girl, in so many ways. It's time to make her mine in one of my favorites.

"Come on." I stand and offer her my hand.

We go inside, but only make it as far as the living room. We just can't control ourselves. I have her on the floor, on the sofa, in the chair by the patio doors. And when afterward she falls asleep, I sneak outside to set up the next piece of our walk down memory lane.

This one is for tomorrow, but it's the most important. It involves not only the past, but also the future.

God, I hope she says yes.

The next day, while Cara is upstairs putting on her bikini, I discard my swim trunks and stretch out on the same lounge chair I was on when she first laid eyes on me.

I make sure everything is the same, down to the way the lounger is positioned in the sun and even how I'm holding my dick. I'm too nervous to get really hard, but when Cara walks out onto the patio and I see her in that skimpy bikini, I'm able to muster a pretty impressive semi.

"Jaxon, what the hell are you doing?" she yells when she sees me start jerking off.

I still my hand and quirk a brow. "Isn't it obvious?"

I think she gets it then.

"Ahh, this is part of our reenactment scenarios, yes?"

"You got it."

"So…" She looks around. "Should I throw a planter at you now or once you really get going?"

Instead of stroking, I wince and cover my junk.

"Uh, I think we'll deviate from the script on that part too. Besides…" I jerk my chin to several blue ceramic shards on the ground. "It looks like one's already been broken."

"Oh my goodness, how did that happen?" Cara's brow crinkles in confusion, but then she realizes I had to be the one to break it. "You did that?" she says.

I nod, and she asks, "But why?"

Sheepishly, I reply, "Well, it was already damaged. And I, uh, was looking at this big crack on the side and accidentally dropped it."

That's mostly the truth, except there was never a crack. I just needed a prop, damn it. So I threw it on the ground, okay? I'm improvising, people!

Suddenly the voice of reason, Miss Plant Thrower herself admonishes, "We shouldn't be busting up Noel's planters, Jaxon."

"Oh, my God." I laugh. "This, from the original pot destroyer."

That makes her blush. "I know, I know. I feel bad about that."

I start to stand, saying, "I guess I should get a dustpan and clean up the mess."

Cara, as I'm hoping, stops me. "No, no, you're naked. You could get cut."

She shudders, and I think I know just what part of me she's most worried about.

"Just stay there, Jaxon. I'll pick up the big pieces, and we can clean up the rest later."

Bending down, she starts gathering the larger shards of blue ceramic.

Perfect!

Cara's playing right into my hands.

When I set this up, I was careful to leave only the pieces that were blunt and couldn't cut her. I tossed the rest away.

Setting aside a handful of shards she's just gathered, she reaches for the final one. It's a big, blue, bowl-shaped piece I turned upside down.

And there's a little something under it.

She flips it over and exclaims, "Jaxon, what the heck is this? Oh my God, I think it's a diamond ring. What's that doing here? And who left it? Oh, wait. Ohhh…"

She gets it then, and I kneel down next to her.

"Cara, I want to ask you something."

I take her hand in mine. I'm already on my knees, so that part's covered.

Clearing my throat, I state as formally as I can, "Will you do me the honor of becoming my wife?"

"Jaxon Holland, are you asking me what I think you're asking?"

I pick up the ring and hold it out to her. "If you think I'm asking you to marry me, then yes."

She throws her arms around me, her bikini-clad body pressed to my naked one, which works wonders for getting me hard as hell now.

"Yes, yes, yes. A thousand times yes, I'll marry you," Cara murmurs into my shoulder.

She said yes! She said yes!

That's all I can think as I lean back and slide the ring onto her finger.

She starts smiling all slyly. And wait, I know that smile.

Still, I ask, "What are you thinking about right now, naughty girl?"

Our gazes meet, and she reaches around and unties her bikini top. It falls away. Next she skillfully shimmies the bottoms off and tosses them aside.

I play dumb. "Uh, babe, not that I'm complaining, but what exactly are you doing?"

"What does it look like I'm doing, Jaxon?"

I raise a brow. "Taking off your bikini so we can have a celebratory fuck?"

"Well, yes, there is that. But I'm also starting a new tradition—naked engagements."

I laugh and pull her into my arms. "I love it, babe. But most of all, I love you."

I do. I so very much do. That's why I know we're going to have such a great life together.

From naked birthdays to naked engagements, from Mr. Hockeypants to Ms. Hockeypants, from the sand to the ice and then back again to the sand, from enemies to friends, from friends to lovers—I just fucking love Cara Milne.

THE END

Next up for the Boys of Winter series is a Brent and Aubrey wedding novella, *Vows on Ice*, due out September 2018. It'll feature all of the couples and follow a series of hilarious mishaps, with an appearance of Area 51, of course. *wink*

Next up after that is a football spin-off featuring Graham Tettersaw, and then we're back to hockey and on to Noel's story!

ABOUT THE AUTHOR

S.R. Grey is an Amazon Top 30 and a #1 Barnes & Noble bestselling author. Her newest bestselling hockey rom-com series features a different hot player in each story and every one can be read in any order since they're all interconnected standalones.

Ms. Grey's novels have appeared on multiple Amazon bestselling lists, including the Top 100 several times. She is also a Top 100 bestselling author on iTunes.

Author Website (stop on by to see how pretty it is):
http://srgrey.com/

S.R. Grey Facebook page is a hoot:
http://www.facebook.com/SRGrey

S.R. Facebook Reading Group is even MORE fun:
https://www.facebook.com/groups/SRGreyHardAbsandHotBooks/

Sign up for S.R. Grey's newsletter (you know you want to):
http://mad.ly/signups/106801/join

S.R. Grey on Twitter (for the random tweets):
https://twitter.com/AuthorSRGrey

S.R. Grey on Instagram for the riveting pics (well, she thinks so):
http://instagram.com/authorsrgrey#

S.R. Grey Goodreads Author page:
http://www.goodreads.com/author/show/6433082.S_R_Grey

It's not over yet.

Here's a chance to read the first chapter of **Resistance on Ice**, Nolan's story and the second standalone in the bestselling *Boys of Winter* series.

SHOCK JOCK ITCH

NOLAN

"**H**ere with us on the air this morning—and it's a hot one out there today, folks—we have with us the man the *Toronto Sun* recently named 'Player to Watch This Upcoming Hockey Season.' You know him as the talented first line right winger for the Las Vegas Wolves. That's right, gang, I'm talking about the *Wolves*, the hockey team that surprised us all in June when they won Lord Stanley's Cup. So, without further ado, please join me in welcoming Mr. Nolan Solvenson."

Radio host Marty Quick turns to me and smiles his trademark cocky, wolfish grin. Damn, this guy may look like a science nerd, what with the bad comb-over and retro horn-rimmed glasses, but he has me beat when it comes to attitude.

Then again, maybe not, since swagger is my middle name.

"Hey, man," he begins, with false sincerity. "Thanks for taking time out of your busy schedule to hang with us this morning. Big congratulations on all your recent successes."

He's being nice enough, but I don't trust him one bit. Everyone knows Marty has a knack for digging up skeletons from your past. And Lord knows mine is a veritable graveyard.

I take a quick swig of the dark roast I picked up from Timmy's on my way here. It was an attempt to fortify myself for this syndicated sports talk radio interview I've resisted all summer. Sadly, even the Tim Horton's coffee I love tastes bitter today.

Forcing a smile, I reply, "Thanks, Marty. I'm happy to be here."

Am I really happy to be here?

Fuck, no!

What kind of crazy fool would purposely place themselves in the line of fire of Canada's own Howard Stern-like shock jock?

Not me.

But my agent insisted. Only because he has no idea of the secrets I have buried. Some are from my distant past, but a few are fairly recent.

One of the not-too-long-ago indiscretions involves the soon-to-be sister-in-law of Brent Oliver, who just happens to be the captain of our team. He would *not* be happy to learn I spent this past winter hooking up with his fiancée's sister. It could be worse, though. Aubrey, Brent's feisty fiancée, might outright kill me if she ever finds out I thoroughly corrupted her sister, Lainey Shelburne.

Okay, Aubrey may not *kill me* kill me, but she'd definitely crush my balls. I wince at the graphic image that conjures up, and Marty Quick eyes me curiously.

The wheels in his head are turning. He suspects I have something to hide. And I do, a lot of things, but I'm not about to share a single one with him.

We break for a commercial and, worried he'll pursue a line of questioning that could land me in hot water when we get back on the air, I try to divert his attention by wincing again. Only this time I make a big show of it, twisting around and stretching my leg out under the table.

"Fucking groin pulls," I mutter, acting all in-pain. "They're a real bitch when you sit for too long."

I don't *really* have a groin pull, nor have I sat for all that long, but ole Marty buys it hook, line, and sinker. We talk about injuries throughout the rest of the break, and when the interview resumes I bring up my summer travels as another good way to keep him off my dick.

"Sounds like you got around a hell of a lot," he says when I review, in great detail, all the places I traveled to during the off-season.

"Yeah, yeah, I did," I confirm.

The more I talk of my international travels, the more I realize this topic isn't such a great idea either. It reminds me of the *reason* why I traveled so much, and that puts me in a solemn mood. Hell, Marty doesn't need another reason to eye me up suspiciously. 'Cause then will come the questions.

Only I need to know my original plan was to spend as much time with Lainey as I could this summer. That plan was shot all to hell, though, when we went our separate ways. That's why I took up traveling the globe.

C'est la vie.

Marty does look at me a little funny when I sigh, but thankfully he just moves on to questions about our Cup run. Since these are easy ones that I've answered a hundred times, I go straight to autopilot. That gives me the chance to mull over how I should've stayed the hell away from Lainey Shelburne in the first place. Though I have to say the cards were stacked against me from day one.

Did I ever really have a chance?

Probably not, since Lainey is simply too gorgeous for any man, including me, to pass by. She's a raven-haired beauty, with the most stunning turquoise eyes, the kind a guy can lose himself in, which I did regularly. And don't even get me started on her curvy little bod.

Yeah, I was a goner from the start.

I also discovered early on that Lainey's—and I really love this one—a freak in the sack. She may very well be the most insatiable girl I've ever had the pleasure of knowing.

And trust me, I've *known* a lot.

I used to think I was high up on the freaky scale, but Lainey's right there with me. Not only does she want sex all the time, any place and any way, but like me, she's into toys and other assorted kink.

In other words, she's my kind of girl.

Too bad we couldn't make it work.

Before the bad shit went down, she and I were not only set to spend the summer together, we were also planning to meet up at Brent and Aubrey's lakehouse in Minnesota. Everything got all blown to hell when I acted like an ass.

Fuck, though, that was then and this is now.

I realize right in that moment, in the middle of this stupid interview, and while answering another playoff run question, that I want Lainey back.

Yes, I do. And I'm going to make it happen, damn it.

Marty finishes up with his Stanley Cup questions, and goes straight to the place that had me dreading this interview in the first place.

"Let's get to the good stuff, Solvenson," he begins, grinning over at me like a perv. "Word on the street is you're quite the ladies' man."

Looking down at the tiny table that separates me from the host in what has taken on the feel of a far too enclosed space, I run my hand through my dark hair. "I don't know about that," I reply. "Rumors are usually just that—rumors."

He's unconvinced, I can tell, but too bad. This is a question I plan to evade like my reputation depends on it. And it may. After I fucked things up with Lainey back in April, I was so distraught that I sought out solace in the form of a slew of strippers.

And I don't mean I found comfort in being with a new one night after night.

Er, though I may have done some of that too.

"Aw, come on," Marty continues in his patented taunting tone. "All of Canada—no, wait, all of North America wants an answer." *Shit, this show does have a far reach.* "Is it true you banged ten strippers in one night?"

I laugh nervously. "No, no, that's not true at all."

It was actually nine and occurred over the course of two days, but who's counting?

Not me. And not anyone else if I have anything to say about it. Besides, the only thing that matters is I'm not technically lying.

See, that's my shtick in life—being clever, outwitting everyone. I'm a wise old sage at the age of twenty-six. My teammates call me things like "sensei" and "Yoda." And, hey, I'm cool with that. Why wouldn't I be? It works out great for me.

That's why if I stick to the gray areas now with Marty, I can successfully evade giving him a straight answer for the next ten minutes, the time left in the interview.

Yeah, you're real clever all right. So clever you outwitted your own damn self with the shit you pulled with Lainey.

"You look a little uneasy there," Shock Jock observes when he sees me frowning. "You sure there's not even a modicum of truth to that stripper story."

"Yep, I'm sure," I snap.

I need to get out of here, and fast. I'm done talking about strippers. And I'm done with this shitty interview. But most of all, I'm done with staying away from Lainey. It's time we have a talk—a *real* talk.

And if talking doesn't work, I'll do what I do best—fuck her till she agrees to start seeing me again.